The
ABSENT
Lord

Jason Beacon

GUERILLA

www.guerillabooks.com

First published in Great Britain in 2013 by Guerilla

Names, characters and related indicia are copyright and trademark
Copyright © 2013 Jason Beacon

Jason Beacon has asserted his moral rights
to be identified as the author

A CIP Catalogue of this book is available from
the British Library

ISBN: 978-1-907248-12-2

CHANDLER®
BOOK DESIGN

Created by
www.chandlerbookdesign.co.uk

Printed and bound in Great Britain
by Ashford Colour Press Ltd.

"Neither do men light a candle, and put it under a bushel, but on a candlestick; and it giveth light unto all that are in the house"

Matthew Ch5 V.15

"It is better to light one small candle than to curse the darkness"

Confucius

"When someone asks what there is to do, light the candle in his hand"

Rumi

1

I T WAS THE fifth of January. Marcus Grool stood, vacant and dull as a tarnished candlestick, on the curb of the street corner and stared. From his left hand dangled a briefcase; in his right, a tightly furled umbrella. From high above, fat, twinkling raindrops tumbled merrily down around the city and some, falling with almost guided precision, splashed noisily onto Marcus Grool's unmoving nose before spattering across his expensive leather shoes.

Marcus Grool's left eye twitched. To the smartly dressed observers who now hurried past in search of shelter or a taxi home, the man standing on the street corner appeared to neither care nor notice as the steady downpour stained his crisp, lined suit a darker shade of grey. The traffic lights jarred from green to red and back; spray from the wheels of cars hissed angrily across his already sodden shins. Still, he remained immobile. Of course, what no one else whizzing by that statuesque anomaly at that moment could know — indeed, what Marcus Grool himself did not know — was that after this day, nothing in his life would ever look the same again.

Marcus Grool arrived home to the small but neatly ordered apartment where he lived with his girlfriend, Elizabeth. Slamming the door behind him, he flung briefcase, umbrella and sopping suit jacket to the sitting room floor before marching across to the fridge. He plucked out a dewy can of beer, cursing as he did the weather for its personal vendetta against him, and then noticed, draining the icy liquid half-empty in one, long gulp, a note on the counter Elizabeth had left him. It said she would be working later than usual tonight but that she would be home in time for dinner. She hoped he had had a good day. It was signed, as ever, with three kisses.

Marcus Grool snorted and kicked off his shoes as he and what remained of his beer went over to the couch and made themselves comfortable. The TV controller fell automatically to hand and for a few minutes he idled disinterestedly through the channels. Irritated by the images before him, he finally flicked the machine off. He finished the beer. The aluminium can made a satisfying scrunching sound in his fist. He leaned forward and placed it on the coffee table. As he did so, he noticed a book he had not seen before. It must have been one Elizabeth was reading, for it was a book about meditation. Aside from at his desk or in front of the television, sitting still was not a pursuit that appealed to Marcus Grool. He flipped over to the back cover and scanned through the blurb. Then he looked again at the photograph on the front.

The author's portrait smiled back, serene and full of calm.

Marcus Grool reached back and, with all his force, hurled the book at the sitting room window. With a boom and a rattle from the pane, the book bounced off the glass, flipped over the lamp and landed, face up and still smiling, in the armchair by the coffee table. Marcus Grool stared for maybe four or even five whole seconds. Then, he threw back his head, closed his eyes, and emptied his lungs at the swirly, white ceiling.

'Argh!' he yelled. He beat his hands on the cushions beside him and jumped up and down. 'Arrgghh!' He smacked at his forehead with the heel of his palm as though trying to burst a bongo drum. Finally, when all the energy from the moment had been spent, Marcus Grool flopped wetly back across his nice, cream sofa and gently began to cry.

'Hello?' The front door banged shut. Across the partly obscured doorway to the bedroom, a petite, frizzy-haired figure blinked past. There was the "click" of the kettle.

'Sorry I'm so late, my love,' the voice continued. It strained as high heels were squeezed from aching feet. 'Some of these parents don't stop talking. I don't know why they send their kids to school in the first place. They all seem to know about teaching. And there's homework to mark already.' There was a pause. 'Marcus?' No reply. Slowly, the bedroom door brushed open against the carpet. The pretty, inquisitive face of Elizabeth appeared in the room. Inquisitiveness became concern. 'Marcus?' she said again.

Marcus Grool sat cross-legged and blank-faced on the bed with an enormous pair of scissors in his hand. Strewn around him, and hanging unevenly from the wardrobe door, were the neatly cut strips of cotton and cloth that had until recently been his suits for work. He wore blue underpants and charcoal socks, and wrapped about his head was a yellow, paisley necktie, which appeared alone in surviving the massacre. A crumple of empty beer cans lay piled beside the bed. He stared at his girlfriend flatly.

'So: we're studying to be a tailor?' said Elizabeth gamely.

'They fired me,' Marcus responded. His voice was devoid of spirit, save for perhaps a trace of beer.

'Oh, baby.' Elizabeth sidled her light form up close to him on the bed and took him in her arms. He sat there limply – like the schoolboy who thinks he has mislaid his sweets, only to discover the dog has swallowed the lot. 'How did that happen?' Elizabeth continued, stroking his hair. 'You said there weren't going to be any more layoffs.'

'It shouldn't have been me,' Marcus said sullenly. 'It should've been Tom Leckle. I work twice as hard as Tom Leckle.'

'What? You mean they kept Tom instead of you? Oh, that's just crazy. Crazy,' repeated Elizabeth. She rocked him gently.

'Yeah, well Tom plays golf at weekends, doesn't he? Down at the clubhouse, chatting up Sir Michael while I put in the overtime. I practically run that department. And there's him, with that facetious smile and the "What a good birdie you got on Saturday, Sir Michael". Makes me sick. I'm going to sue for unfair dismissal, I tell you, that's what I'm going to do.'

'I could always give you golf lessons as a late Christmas present?' suggested Elizabeth, smiling. But Marcus just grunted and pushed her away.

'Why won't you take me seriously?' He pulled the necktie irritably from his head and hoisted himself off the bed to stand in the doorway. 'This isn't a game, you know, Elizabeth? This is my life — our lives. On the line.' He stared at her for a second longer. Then he turned and went into the bathroom, closing the door behind him.

Elizabeth sighed heavily. She looked down at her tired feet and rubbed them, thinking of all the homework she still had left to mark.

So: finally it had happened. She supposed she should feel sorry, or worried at least. Yet, as she sat there cross-legged on the bed, Elizabeth was slightly surprised to find that more than anything she felt a great sense of relief. Next door in the living area, the kettle rumbled to the boil and clicked itself off. She caught her reflection in the mirror. Was she surprised, she asked it? The reflection frowned. Then Elizabeth took a deep breath and got up to go and make herself some coffee in readiness for her work. Either way, it was going to be a hard, cold winter.

'I'm sorry. Beth? Bethy.' Marcus stood there in his bath towel. Feebly, he raised an imploring hand.

At the long, high counter that divided the living room from the kitchen, Elizabeth carried on writing. Her other hand propped her head up beneath straying, curly tresses. She sniffed.

Marcus dropped his hand to his side. 'Bethy: come on.'

'I've got work to do, Marcus,' said Elizabeth, not raising her eyes.

'I said I'm sorry. I didn't mean to snap again. I've had a really bad day.' He shuffled and poked at a bit of fluff he had noticed on the carpet by his foot. Frowning, he bent and picked it up. 'I know, I know, the beer doesn't help.' He walked behind her to dispose of the offending loose fibres. 'It's just a bad start to the year, that's all. It'll be all right. I know some people. Tomorrow I'll ask around. I'll…' Marcus stopped, unsure.

Elizabeth put down her pen. 'I know you will,' she said. She smiled weakly. She heaved another big sigh. 'But it's not just the job, is it, Marcus? I thought we'd been through this — haven't we?'

The other blinked. 'I don't know what you mean.'

'Everything!' Elizabeth cried suddenly, throwing up her hands. 'Marcus, it's everything, isn't it? You against the world — these are your plans, this is where you're going, this is how we get there. It's all about you. And if it works it's because you're a genius and if it doesn't it's because life's unfair. What's not fair, Marcus? The world revolving around Marcus Grool? There's a child of eight in one of my classes, his work's been bad lately. Do you know what I found out this evening? What Father Christmas brought this year?'

'Bethy…'

'A father with three months to live, Marcus. They can't afford medical insurance and because of the fraud that is this country's health service, he can't be treated. That's where the "not fair" line gets off. Why is it always about you?'

'Bethy.' Holding his ground, Marcus raised a forefinger. 'Just listen to me for a second. I'm very sorry to hear about this child, but the only future we have any control over is our own.'

'Cah…' Elizabeth dropped down off her stool and strode past him. She fell back onto the sofa, knees tucked beneath her slim body. Her boyfriend rotated impotently where he stood, half-naked, in his towel. There may not have been much to the young schoolteacher physically but when she burned, she blazed.

'Who do you think I've been doing this for? Who?' he demanded. There was no answer. 'For us, Bethy. For both of us – for our future. Don't you understand? That job was going places, it was…it was going to make us.' He coughed. 'But there's no use getting all emotional about it. Some tired, kitchen drama re-enactment doesn't do anyone any good, we know that. I got a severance pay. That'll keep me going until something comes along.'

'How much?' asked Elizabeth quietly.

Marcus shifted and looked down at his bare chest. 'Ten thousand.' The other pursed her lips and raised her eyebrows but said nothing. 'If I invest it properly,' continued Marcus, 'then maybe I'll be able…. Bethy? What are you doing?'

Elizabeth was moving again, this time towards her handbag. Marcus watched, puzzled and silent as she went through her purse. Eventually, she pulled out a card. She held it out briskly and without a word. He took it with a degree of wariness. The card was lined and faded. Marcus flipped it over in his fingers.

Across the centre, in old-fashioned, calligraphic letters were the words:

Dr Edmond Ummond – Q.U.A.C.K.

Underneath were an address and telephone number.

Marcus looked up. He regarded his girlfriend's eyes coldly – and with a flicker of fear. 'I don't need to see anyone,' he breathed roughly.

'You need to talk to someone,' Elizabeth said. 'Or just listen, maybe. I don't know.' She watched him, almost shaking before her. Suddenly, she softened and took his hands in her own.

'You're lost, Marcus,' Elizabeth said. Her fingers played

lightly on his. 'You've been away so long, and I don't know how to find you.' She looked at him, and then to the card between their hands. 'A parent at the school recommended him. He's not your usual kind of therapist. Apparently he's...' She paused and bit her lip. 'He has a different approach to most — but very effective. It's not far from here. You'll have plenty of time, now. That is, if you really don't want to take up golf,' she added, glancing up at him.

Marcus hesitated. He flapped the little card in front of him as though it were a distress signal. 'I don't need any of this New Age psychobabble,' he said intently. 'It's my job that's gone missing — not my mind. All I need is to get back on track. You'll see,' he insisted, though he failed to convince either of them. 'If I invest some of the ten thousand –'

'Shh.' Elizabeth placed a finger on his lips. 'Why don't you invest in yourself for a change, hm? Nothing else matters. There's so much more to you than this, Marcus Grool. At least, I used to think there was. Isn't there? Isn't there, Marcus? Because, if there isn't...'

Marcus, however, remained silent. Elizabeth looked at him for a few seconds more, tight-lipped and with a shadow of resignation. There was no need to interpret that look. Marcus swallowed as his girlfriend traced her small fingers over his chest. Then, she turned aside and moved past him.

Picking up her books, Elizabeth switched out the kitchen light and went tiredly towards the bedroom.

Marcus regarded once more the crumpled piece of destiny in his hand.

Dr Edmond Ummond – Q.U.A.C.K.

What an absurd business card, he thought. His features darkened as he cleared his throat. 'How did you know I'd lost my job, anyway?' he asked.

In the doorway to the bedroom, Elizabeth paused. 'I didn't get the card tonight,' she said. She gave him a thin smile. Then, hesitating for just a second, she disappeared.

Marcus Grool blinked and wondered just what he had done to deserve such a very, difficult life.

2

UDSWICK ROAD WAS located in an obscure, quiet part of town, the journey to which took longer than he had anticipated. When Marcus finally did arrive, he frowned and once more fished the card from his coat pocket to be sure. What immediately struck the visitor on first viewing this cosy little street had less to do with *where* it was than the impression given of *when* it was. It was as though the entire high street of some quaint, old market town of a hundred years before had been warped, sounds, smells and all, into the present day. There was a cobbler's, a confectionary, a bookbinder's, a tailor's; the butcher, the baker, the watchmaker. Marcus half-expected any minute to see a horse and carriage come trotting by with frock-coated footmen aboard. The toot of a car horn behind him broke his daydreaming and made him step back onto the curb.

Towards the far end of the street he could just make out an Elizabethan tavern. The heavy, wooden signboard wavered in the blustery January breeze. On the board was painted a magnificent sailing ship and, beneath this, the words: "The Brave Seadreamer". There were no hamburger restaurants, no supermarkets, no homestyle shops and not a single mobile telephone centre in sight. Marcus felt in his other pocket for his own phone just to reassure himself he was still in the right century.

No. 73 was opposite the watchmaker and was perhaps the most singular oddity of them all. It was built from stern and imposing dark stone blocks, as one might encounter in the houses that line the streets of Edinburgh. It consisted of a basement with two high storeys above and gave the authoritative air of a building that could easily have been half the town hall. "Half" is indeed right, for next door – No. 75 – was its exact mirror image, saving the fact that from pavement to roof it had been decorated in soft, pink stucco. A bronze plaque by the door announced it to be some kind of dance school. Gazing up to the roof of the peculiar edifice, Marcus noted a large, glass conservatory, which was bedecked with bursting, colourful hanging baskets in spite of the season, straddling the two addresses.

Marcus frowned. He considered turning around then and there, until the sight of a man passing by in a suit reminded him he had little else to be doing. He looked down at his own attire, which seemed so alien to him on a weekday morning. Then, surprised but not overly curious at his surroundings, he pottered up the short flight of steps to No. 73. Reading up the list of six names by the door, he saw "Dr Edmond Ummond" at the top and pressed the bell. Nothing happened. Looking once more at the card in his hand, he pushed again and then, automatically, tried the brass handle of the flaking, wooden door. The pointed metal was cold in his grasp. It yielded and the door swung silently inward.

Marcus found himself in a reception hall akin to an old, grand hotel lobby. The walls were papered in patterned silk, the furniture decorated in velvet; the floorboards were varnished almost black and there was a distinct touch of woodworm to the main desk. A creaky looking staircase dog-legged back upon itself towards the high ceiling above. No one was about. Marcus called tentatively into the spacious hallway but no answer came. Just as he was deciding to give up on the whole, stupid idea, a colossal voice – held in place by an equally proportioned lady – whirled through a nearby doorway and, with a heave of breath, plumped itself down behind the desk.

'Oh my,' exclaimed the old dame, flummoxed and smiling all at once. She had bright, round cheeks and sparkly light-blue buttons for eyes. Her hair was tied up in a tight, white bun and her accent came straight from a cider press. She flicked through a leather appointments book before her. Then, giving up, she beamed up at the visitor before her. 'I'll bet you're Marcus Grool,' she said, squinting slyly. 'We talked on the telephone.'

'Er, yes. Yes, we did,' replied Marcus, uncontrollably smiling back.

'Ah, ain't you a handsome devil – just like I said you'd be? I can tell these things, you know?'

'Mm,' replied Marcus, nodding uncertainly. He looked down. Seeing the card still between his fingers, he said: 'I've come to see the quack.'

The quirky old receptionist chuckled coyly at herself and covered her mouth with a pudgy hand. 'There I go again,' she laughed. Then, sobering, she said: 'Half a tock, now. I'll just let Dr Ummond know you're here.' She whispered rapidly into the receiver of the old-fashioned telephone. Having finished, she smiled up once more. 'The Doctor'll be ready just as soon as,' she told him affably. 'Well now. Can I be taking your coat for you?'

'Oh, no. That's fine. Thank you,' said Marcus.

The receptionist hefted her cracking bulk to its feet. 'Hot cup of tea?' she panted, smiling her way over to the door through which she had first bowled. 'Kettle's boiled just this instant.'

'No, really,' insisted Marcus. 'I'll just...' He cleared his throat. 'I'll just wait.'

The other shrugged. 'All right, then. Have it your way. You can go up now, if you like. First floor.'

'Really? I thought you said -' Marcus frowned. Then he coughed and said: 'Well. Thank you.' He started up the stairs.

'Good luck, now,' added the receptionist, watching him as he went. A strange, sudden tone of *somethingness* in her voice made Marcus hesitate and turn around. The old woman gave him a quick, little wink. Then, she was gone.

"Dr Edmond Ummond – *Q*uintessentially *U*nique *A*nd *C*ertainly *K*lever" as proclaimed by the sign on the door of the study, lay spread-eagled in his chair with his head back, snoring loudly. Marcus approached the desk with a certain degree of caution. Leaning from the waist, he peered gingerly over at the occasionally twitching form of the so-called "cutting edge" doctor of psychiatry.

For a start, he was old. At least in his seventies, Marcus surmised, if not older. He studied with disdain the sallow skin, the dry lips and the electric shock of long white hair that immediately characterised the sleeping man. He was also as lean as a one-legged stork and was unfashionably dressed in a baggy and threadbare chocolate, corduroy suit. A red silk handkerchief fluttered from his breast pocket and, as the visitor looked closer, he noticed with a sense of revulsion the hairs of the other man's nostrils fidgeting excitedly on the strength of his breathing. To cap it all, there was more gold showing in the gaping, ancient mouth than there was ivory.

Marcus straightened. What had been bemusement was now irritation, possibly annoyance, even. He glanced perfunctorily about the room. Everything was antique, belonging to a bygone age: from the heavy wooden chest and mahogany closet that stood respectively against the walls nearest the door, to the thick, sashed curtains at the window and the five-pronged candelabra on the desk. Past their best before date, like the old shrink himself, snorted Marcus privately. A broken cuckoo clock on the mantelpiece behind the desk held eternity at seventeen minutes to six. The little wooden bird gaped blindly into space from the end of a rusty spring.

'Hello? Dr Ummond? Doctor?' Marcus received no response but the faintest, unconscious passing of wind. He pulled his overcoat from where he had draped it neatly over one arm. 'Right, that does it,' he muttered crossly. He'd tell Elizabeth a thing or two about this, that was for sure. He made ready to leave.

'Zeek zooks!' In a flash, the old man was awake and rigid in his chair. His hair stood out from his skull at right-angles and he stared wildly about. He threw a glance at the cuckoo clock behind him. 'Holy crumpet,' he exclaimed to himself. 'That's where the time goes, Ummond, you great fool. Up, awake! To business!' The Doctor blinked and looked about the apparently empty room. One long, white eyebrow arched acutely. 'Now that's a funny thing,' he muttered, smacking his thin lips together.

From behind the far edge of the great, wooden desk, the figure of Marcus Grool inexorably emerged into the good Doctor's view. 'I'm here,' he said, rising slowly from his knees. The force of the other man's eruption had sent him cowering to the floor. He regarded Dr Ummond now with wary suspicion, and little warmth. 'I'm Marcus Grool,' he stated flatly.

'Are you, indeed?' Edmond Ummond surveyed his visitor with a narrow, steady gaze. His eyes were a pellucid sea-green. They were the sort of eyes that age can never dim. Within them resided the memories of many a long-watched Moon.

The Doctor looked Marcus quickly up and down. Then, waving a long hand, he sat himself back in his chair. 'Well, I suppose it's not your fault,' he said dismissively. 'What do you want?'

Marcus motioned towards the chair. Receiving no further invitation, he seated himself opposite. He cleared his throat. 'Well, actually, my girlfriend made me come and see you, really,' he said. 'I, er…I lost my job, you see, and I suppose I've been a bit. Well: down.'

Dr Ummond grunted into his chest and fixed his eyes pointedly on Marcus' own from beneath his lined forehead. Without shifting his attention, he reached into a drawer by his right hand and picked out a tall, white candle. This he placed in a candlestick on the desk. With his other hand, eyes still unmoving, he patted about the desktop, and subsequently in his jacket pockets until finally, with a cluck of satisfaction, he procured a tatty box of matches. The Doctor struck a match, which fizzed loudly, and put it carefully to the candle. His eyes had not flickered. Dr Ummond sat back in his chair.

'Ahem, yes, well,' began Marcus again, unsure. 'Shall I? Yes, all right then. So anyway: I lost my job, as I said, which was a blow, um, especially seeing as really it was an unfair dismissal. And then Elizabeth – my girlfriend – well, she gets quite over-emotional sometimes, a bit worked up, you know?'

Marcus continued to speak as the Doctor regarded him in silence. He told him about Elizabeth and the argument they had had and then, without really noticing or intending to, about the suit incident and his anger at the injustice of the whole situation. After a few minutes had gone by, the old man opposite said suddenly, quietly but with clear enunciation: 'This isn't going to be another one about sex, is it?'

Marcus blinked to a halt. 'Excuse me?'

'You know: sex. The old wrestle with the pestle.' He spoke out of the corner of his mouth.

Marcus shifted uncomfortably in his chair. 'No, it – not at all.' He clutched his overcoat in his lap.

'Good,' pronounced Dr Ummond severely. He banged the desk with his long, fine fingers. 'You don't know how very tired I get of listening to young men's problems about sex. There's only ever two problems men have with sex. Do you know what they are, laddie?'

Marcus stalled, then shook his head. 'No.'

'It won't go up' – the Doctor jabbed a finger at the ceiling – 'or, and which is usually by far the graver case' – he stamped on the floor – 'it won't go down. And in my experience there's nothing one man can say to another as will make the slightest bit of difference. Now carry on.'

Slightly dazed, Marcus stammered back onto the thread from which he had been diverted. Again, the Doctor appeared to listen, only this time he was anything but still. He drummed on the arms of his chair, opened and closed drawers noisily, fiddled with his handkerchief. Finally, making curious, unintelligible utterances under his breath, he stood up with a frown and walked stiffly to the corner of the room, whereupon he opened a small door that Marcus had not noticed previously. There was the sound of a light switch being flicked on. Moments later, he distinctly heard the stream of water into a bowl.

Marcus paused. So too, it seemed, did the Doctor. 'Anyway,' Marcus began once more, 'If she could just see the situation from my perspec-'

'Ahhh,' went Dr Ummond, and began to cackle as the sound of falling water once again reached Marcus' ears.

'Listen, Doctor, if this isn't-'

'Go on, go on, zeeks squeaks,' said the old man, waving a hand back into the room. Marcus caught a glimpse of the evidently deranged psycho-pensioner as, to the accompaniment of flushing, he wandered across the light source beyond. The next thing he knew, he heard the unmistakable burr and hum of an old, electric razor. A couple of minutes later, the light clicked off and Ummond re-entered the room.

'Look, I don't want to be rude,' said Marcus Grool as the other re-seated himself and probed at his chin, 'but I don't believe you're taking me very seriously.'

'Hah!' Ummond rocked back in his chair. He slapped a thin leg and chortled to himself, licking his tongue over his long, yellow and gold teeth as he did. A second later, he snapped back, deadpan. 'I take everything seriously,' he said. Then, with a slight curl of the lip he added: 'Except for people.'

'Except?'

'That's right.'

'Then why..?'

'I have diagnosed your problem,' Ummond said casually. He inspected a well cared for fingernail.

'You have?'

'Assuredly,' replied the Doctor.

Marcus waited. 'So?' he blurted. 'What is it?'

Dr Ummond did not regard him as he said: 'You are not at home.'

Marcus blinked furiously. He looked down at his overcoat and then, with a frown, said: 'But…'

'Listen!' cried the Doctor, suddenly pouncing forward so that he was almost halfway across the desk to the astonished Grool. He planted a bony elbow and aimed his finger like a pistol sight between the other man's eyes. His own pupils were wide and terrifying. 'You (he emphasised the word) are not at home.'

There was a charged pause as the two men stared at one another. Marcus gulped. 'What is that?' he asked, an edge to his voice. 'More New Age rubbish?' His eyes narrowed.

'Hah,' squawked Ummond, retreating once again.

He exhaled with a whistle through his teeth. 'New Age,' he repeated. 'He calls it New Age. Oh dear.'

'Look: if by any incredibly slim chance you do know something about this, I would appreciate it if you told me,' asserted Marcus, trying to hold on to his temper.

Ummond looked puzzled. 'But I just did tell you,' he said.

'I mean' – Marcus searched for the word – 'specifically.'

The Doctor shook his head and then, scratching it for good measure, pushed himself up from his chair and wandered over to the window. 'Always the same,' he muttered, placing his hands on his narrow hips and absently surveying the street below. 'They come asking questions, and if you don't give them the answer they were expecting, they ask for the one they were till your ears drop off.'

'I thought you people were supposed to be scientific.' Marcus stared with frustration at the Doctor's eccentric silhouette.

'Zooks!' exclaimed Ummond. 'Scientific, eh?' He smacked his forehead before wheeling about. 'In Sixteen hundred they had a science called "burning witches".' He advanced on the befuddled Grool. 'What d' ya think they'll say about modern psychiatry in four hundred years, huh? The less the better, I hope. Tell me, Grool' – Ummond hung over him, wraith-like: 'What is there new under the Sun?'

'You can't take that line.' Marcus looked up into the other's crazed expression and did his best to swallow subtly. 'That's just your trouble. You're stuck in the past, you haven't – you haven't evolved. I mean, look at this place.'

'New Age or anachronism, you can't have it both ways,' said Ummond. He ambled back around the desk and slumped into his chair with a sigh. His eyes flicked up sharply. 'Schoolteacher, you say?'

'What?'

'Your missy.'

'Yes, but-'

'Teaches young kids, does she?' Dr Ummond arched an eyebrow.

'Yes,' said Marcus slowly.

'Then perhaps you should join one of her classes. There's obviously not much I can do.' He dipped a finger in the molten wax of the candle and brought it to his nose for closer inspection.

'I came here,' grated Marcus, as near close to boiling as ever, 'for some help.'

'Then you're in the wrong place,' snapped the Doctor. 'You can't give help to anyone. Most especially not to helpless men like you who haven't even got the gee-up to have an honest-to-God sex problem. My line is guidance, but if you're determined to spend your life in the sewer you might at least find the courage to be a proper rat. Good day.'

Marcus rose, trembling, to his feet. 'I'm leaving,' he announced through clenched teeth.

'Now that's funny – I could have sworn I heard someone squeak,' said Ummond, looking perplexedly about the carpet. In a single, swift movement, he snuffed out the candle on the desk with the palm of his hand.

At the door, Marcus halted momentarily. He frowned; hesitated. There was something very unsettling about that seemingly insignificant gesture. Marcus could not define it, but it made him go suddenly cold. 'Why did you do that?'

'Oh, you still here? If I told you you'd only want another answer anyway. You know your trouble, Grool?' said the Doctor, leaning back until he was almost horizontal: 'You're too thin.'

At that, the younger man turned on his heel and strode indignantly out of the study.

'What d' you reckon, Doc?' said Ummond to himself when the other had gone. 'Three days?' He nodded. 'All right, Edmond, my boy: you're on. Three it is.'

Outside in the cold, Marcus began to pace furiously towards the bus stop at the end of the street. He had never been so incensed in all his life – not even when his boss had fired him. If there was one thing for certain, it was that he never wanted to see Ludswick Road, with its weird old shops and barmy receptionists, and above all that crazy old madman, ever again in his life. Who on Earth did he think he was, speaking to him in that way? What right did he have? Marcus heard a window slide open, somewhere behind and above him.

'Marcus Grool, he's such a fool,

Better catch up, he's late for school;

Marcus Grool, he's such a fool…' went the taunting refrain.

Marcus neither turned nor hesitated, but continued to march stoically onward, scowling, until the doodle-ally Doctor was finally out of earshot.

Edmond Ummond watched him go with his sharp, sea-green eyes. A smattering of people had stopped in the street below and now stood squinting up at the white-haired gentleman where he perched on his windowsill. Ummond looked down at them and waved merrily. Across the way, Mr Meztchek, the watchmaker, was standing in his shop's entrance, hands in apron, watching. The Doctor caught his regard. He winked at him.

The watchmaker nodded knowingly. Then, with a chuckle and a smile, he returned to his dealings with time.

*   *   *

'How did it go with Dr Ummond?' Elizabeth asked innocently as the door boomed shut and Marcus stormed into the apartment.

'I've not been spoken to like that in my entire life,' said Marcus, biting the words as he hurled his overcoat across the armchair. He paced and fumed. 'He is the rudest, the craziest, the most insolent, ignorant human being I have ever had the misfortune to meet.'

Elizabeth did not look up from where she was cracking eggs into a bowl in the kitchen. 'Well then,' she said, switching on the whisk. 'Sounds as though maybe you shouldn't go back.'

'Oh, don't you worry,' Marcus swore, 'I won't. If there's one thing you can be quite sure of — I won't.'

3

'MR GROOL! HOW nice to have you back again.'

Marcus smiled uncertainly at the radiating old receptionist. It was not the welcome he had imagined. 'I, er. . .'

'Oh, to see the Doctor again, yes of course,' said the other, giggling to herself. 'He is a special one, isn't he?'

'Yes,' replied Marcus. 'Yes, I guess you could say.'

The smiling old lady waddled past him with a twinkle. 'Kettle's just boiled, if you fancy.'

Marcus shook his head. 'Thanks anyway.'

'All right, then. Well up you go.' She disappeared next door. Marcus raised his eyebrows at the empty space. Then, slowly he went upstairs.

'Blast and drat! Well get it, man, get it!' The excited voice of Dr Ummond reached Marcus' ears from halfway down the landing outside the little study. There was a sound of scuffling and agitation. 'There! Right there! Where are your eyes, man?' Marcus heard another's voice mumble an apology. He smiled to himself as the Doctor evidently lost all patience and ordered the other man, accompanied by a brief but incisive personal analysis, firmly out of the room. A moment later, the focus of the Doctor's irritation — an elderly gentleman in a neatly pressed suit — emerged from the study with a handful of what appeared to be small bits of metal held disdainfully before him. He nodded formally to the visitor as he passed and then disappeared through the door at the end of the landing. Marcus advanced and poked his head into the room.

'Hello?'

'Zeeks!' Ummond's face snapped up. 'Ah, Grool, my boy. Here, quick: come and put your finger on this.' Marcus approached the desk. Scattered across its surface in a hundred pieces or more was the mechanism for what appeared to be an old-fashioned pocket watch. He placed his finger on the part indicated by the Doctor. With his long, purple tongue reaching almost around to one ear, the Doctor then carefully took a spring between a pair of tweezers and attempted to fit it delicately into the assemblage. The spring pinged out and hit the old man square between the eyes.

'Drat and blast!' he exclaimed once more. 'Ah well. Never mind.' He nodded to Marcus, who stepped back and sat himself down. Then, with a single sweep, Ummond cleared all the tiny cogs and wheels into the drawer at his side and closed it firmly shut. He patted his suit pockets, frowning, and then, as though remembering something, he lightened and hinged his frail form back into his chair. He stared at the young man before him. 'So,' he declared after a silence. He smacked his lips. 'You've come back.'

'Yes. I mean – I have,' replied Marcus, shifting.

'I see.' The old man's gaze was like rock. He stuck a finger in his tufty left ear and gave it a waggle. 'So what made you come back to a mad old quack like me, eh?'

Marcus' brow furrowed. 'Well,' he said. He coughed, and scratched at his temple. 'Well,' he said again. 'That's just it. I'm not sure, really.'

'That's right, you're not. You're Grool.'

'I think it might be something you said possibly about help and guidance,' Marcus continued. 'You know – not being the same thing. What's the difference?'

As Marcus had been speaking, Dr Ummond had once more succeeded in locating his box of matches and had relit the candle on the desk, which had not moved since the previous session. He reclined again and contemplated, his white hair waving gently like an anemone above his head. 'What's the difference, he says, eh? Hmm. Won the bet, though, didn't I, you rascal? That'll remind you. I don't know,' he said finally, turning to Marcus. 'Go and ask the Bible, it's beyond me. How's the teacher?'

'How's the..? She's -' Marcus flustered. 'I thought we were here to talk about me,' he managed hotly.

Dr Ummond studied his visitor scrupulously. 'Have you got something against me, Grool?' he asked slowly. ''Cause if you have I think we'd better hear it pronto, d' ya understand?'

Marcus thought. He felt that familiar sensation of agitation rising once again. It had been a foolish decision to come back here, he saw that now. What could have made him do it? He looked at the candle on the desk, burning innocently away. The candle seemed to look back at him. There was almost something about it – something that made something else inside of him, Marcus Grool, strain to make a connection. But the connection would not be made. Exasperated, he looked helplessly at the ever-watchful Doctor. 'It's the cliché,' he said exhaustively.

'The what?'

Marcus waved a hand. 'You, this office: everything. The old, wacky, quack.'

'Oh.' Ummond crinkled approvingly.

'It's so utterly tired and familiar,' the young man continued, 'so passé — but at the same time being here is totally alien to me. Maybe that's why I came back. Maybe I just need the change.' Marcus rambled to a sorry halt.

The Doctor got up quietly. Moving with a little difficulty, he walked around behind him. 'If something's a cliché, lad,' he whispered, 'it's for a reason. Often the reason is because it contains some of that truth nonsense. So,' he said, patting the other's shoulder and completing a full circle of the desk, 'always look twice when you meet a cliché. You with it? Now answer me: what is there that's new under the Sun?'

Marcus regarded the Doctor grumpily for a second, then thought. Eventually, half with a look of satisfaction, he said: 'Computers.'

'Hah!' shrieked Dr Ummond. 'Computers, he says. That fat thing,' he cried, pointing, 'that is unfortunately attached to your neck, is the oldest computer in the world. People used to be able to store thousands of lines of poetry in there — build temples in it that reached to the Moon. Nowadays, with all these fancy plastic imitations about, it barely gets used. Nothing to do all day except dream, and dream.' He covered his eyes theatrically with his skinny hand as though calling on the muse.

Marcus sat and thought for a moment of all the plans

he had had before he was fired. All his dreams. Now, they were gone. 'You've got to have dreams,' he said fixedly. 'You have to have something to aim for.'

'Well for sure,' responded Ummond. He regarded him cannily. 'Just as long as you know when you're dreaming.'

The young man frowned. He pulled himself straight again in his chair. 'All right. So there is nothing new under the Sun,' he said compliantly.

'Nothing,' agreed the Doctor. 'Except for man.' On this occasion, Marcus did not even attempt a response. He sat and regarded the old crackpot blankly. 'How long,' Ummond went on, scratching his nose, 'do you suppose it takes the Sun to take a breath?'

'To do..?'

'You know: breathing.' He wheezed asthmatically in and out. 'Something you can do to remember you're alive.'

'I don't know,' Marcus replied tightly.

'Three million years. The entire history of humanity?' Again, no reply. He snapped his fingers. 'Less than a blink. And you, Mr Marcus Grool, even if you live to be threescore years and twenty – will barely be noticed.'

'What does this have to do with anything?' Marcus asked.

'Zeek zooks,' exclaimed the Doctor. 'You really take some stirring up, Grool. All right. I'll tell you a secret. I suppose I'll just have to trust you. The only reason man is new to the Sun is on account of his dreams. You follow?'

Marcus struggled. 'The Sun doesn't understand consciousness?' he proffered at length.

At that remark, the ancient Doctor practically self-combusted. 'No, you great blundering, oatmeal blancmange!' he cried. 'Precisely the opposite! It's *un*consciousness that's so totally, fantastically newfangled. What did I tell you last time – you are not at home? You're out playing golf while your servants run amok. Don't you ever get tired of whacking your little white balls pointlessly all over the blessed countryside?'

The recipient of this barrage remained curiously tight-lipped as he measured out the words: 'I don't play golf.'

The Doctor calmed himself. 'You don't, eh?' He clicked his tongue and then, with a mutter, wandered over to the window. He placed his hands on his hips as ever and took in the wintry street below him. It was quiet, and quite peaceful; generally no different from the way it always was. Edmond Ummond's sea-green eyes flicked from left to right. They narrowed a little, and he allowed himself the corner of a smile. 'Do you know what is meant by the phrase "to be Lord of your castle", Grool?' he asked quietly without turning.

'Lord of?' Marcus steadied himself, determined to keep his temper under control. 'No, I believe I don't,' he replied evenly.

'Every man and woman on this Earth,' continued Ummond, speaking as though to himself, 'is a castle, you see, my lad? And every castle needs a master to preside over it. That all might sound very illiberal to you, I know. Well does it?' Marcus shrugged. 'No matter.' The Doctor sucked his teeth. 'We all like to think we invented the rules. But a castle without its Lord is a castle destined for ruin, and there's no other way around the fact, you'd better believe it. Tell me,' said Ummond slowly, face turned still towards the window: 'Did you ever hear the story of the Absent Lord?' He swung about suddenly with surprising composure and fixed the blinking Marcus Grool.

'I — I don't believe…'

'Good,' interrupted the Doctor. 'Then you're gonna hear it because it might just tickle you right. That's if,' he added, pausing suddenly by the fireplace as he re-crossed the room, 'you've got the lolly.' He arched a long eyebrow. The other hesitated. 'Come on, Grool,' Ummond snapped, returning to the desk. 'What colour's your money?'

'Well…how much do you charge?' asked Marcus.

'A thousand an hour.'

'A thousand?!' the other stammered.

'That's right,' affirmed Ummond. 'If you don't pay for it you'll never appreciate it. Besides, I could do with some new rags to boot.' As if for emphasis, he stuck his finger through a hole in his jacket and gave it a wiggle.

'I understand that, of course,' Marcus blustered. 'It's just that I...that is, I...'

'Ahh, I've got it: you thought I was cheap, didn't you?' sniffed the Doctor.

'Not cheap, exactly, only -'

'Well I'm not,' the other snapped, closing the matter. 'People spend fortunes on televisions and fancy kitchens; holidays they come back from with nothing to show for except a missing layer of skin. But when it comes to the only thing that might make a real difference to their lives' – he drew an imaginary zip across the top of his pockets – 'tight as a Scotsman on Burns Night. There you have it, Grool. If you wanna stay' – he grinned wickedly – 'you gotta pay.'

Marcus thought desperately. He had saved a little money over the last few years – and of course, there was his severance pay, which had just cleared into his account. But that was supposed to be used for investing in something firm, like shares or even property. Elizabeth would not know anything about it until one day, he could surprise her by declaring: "We're rich". And on that day, she would see he'd been right all along and any troubles between them would disappear. As long as he found another job, of course. In the two days since he had first met the mad Doctor, the prospects did not look promising. He frowned and coughed into his fist. 'How long does this, er, *story* go on for?' Marcus asked.

Ummond gleamed. 'For ever,' he said. Then he waved an arm. 'Very well, Grool. You lost your job and your girlfriend thinks you're an aphid — you're pulling all my strings. I tell you what: I'll make you a deal.' He drew the last word out across blackened gums. 'See this candle?' he said, turning it towards the prospective patient. 'It's ten hours long.'

Marcus leaned forward to inspect. For the first time, he noticed a scale in delicate, black Roman numerals, running from "I" just short of the top of the candle down to the figure "X" near the bottom. The flame continued to burn.

'This is how it works,' explained the Doctor. 'If we haven't got you on the right track before the hot bit reaches ten, you get the lot for free. If, on the other hand, some miracle occurs halfway through and you want to go tell the world what's who, you pay the time you used. Or,' he concluded, 'you give me £278 and ninepence this instant before you skeet straight out the door. Take a choice.'

Marcus looked up. 'How can you be so precise?'

'I've done a lot of work with candles,' replied the other. 'Well, pilgrim? What'll it be?'

Marcus Grool took a long, deep breath. A hundred thoughts and images flickered through his head and

38

somewhere beneath it all, for the first time in a very long while, was just the merest pang of excitement. The unknown called out his name. Resolutely setting his jaw, he thrust his arm across the desk and said: 'Done'.

'Weh-hey!' cried the Doctor, jumping up and shaking the outstretched hand with vigour. 'We'll make porridge of you yet, Grool. Now: where's that tailor's number got to?'

Marcus could feel his heart pounding in his chest. He grinned bashfully, then his face fell suddenly serious. 'I will be able to get a tax receipt, won't I?'

'Don't you worry,' said Ummond calmly, rifling through his desk. 'We may be over the hill but we haven't left the planet. Where in God's name did I leave that storybook..?'

'I still don't understand that business about the Sun, though,' Marcus said as he made himself comfortable.

'Drat,' muttered Ummond. 'Nope. Can't find it. I'll just have to – the Sun?' he exclaimed.

'What it's got to do with me coming to see you.'

'Ah yes, the Sun.' Dr Ummond looked at the young man slyly. 'Do you know why it shines so very hot and bright upon us?' he asked. 'Even though we people make it choke?' Marcus frowned, unknowing. The Doctor beamed. 'It shines, my erstwhile young partner, because everyone needs a light to follow. Now listen.'

4

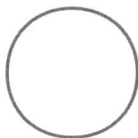

'ONCE UPON A time there was a handsome young Lord. He lived with his servants in a beautiful castle by the woods in the mysterious land of Ude.'

'Is it all going to be like this?' broke in Marcus.

'Cliché all the way. Three hundred in cash now or are you along for the ride?'

'Sorry.'

'You didn't go to a shrink to listen to Dickens, did you? Now pay attention and keep still. In his castle, the Lord retained five servants. Their names were: Balthazar Grimble, the caretaker; Tooley O' Marge, the cook; Elbows Mick, the mason; Patterson Nitch, the general dogsbody; and...' Ummond paused, suddenly searching. Then his face fell flat. From the side of his mouth, in the fashion only old people can, he pronounced with distaste the word: 'Falego'.

'Falego?'

'The Spanish imp who fed the beasts. But at the time our story starts he was still very young. Don't rupture your brain cell trying to remember them all, you'll know them soon enough.' The Doctor went on:

'Rising from the top of the castle was a tall and mighty tower, and to the sturdy, oak-wood door of this tower the Lord alone held the key. None of the servants was ever allowed up there. For in that tower his Lordship had his workshop. And in this workshop, he used to make candles.

'You might think it curious that a Lord should be a candle maker but for starters, in those days the aristocracy weren't the idle, ineffectual bunch they generally are now, and secondly, these were not your ordinary candles. He could make candles of any size or form, any smell or colour, that you could ever possibly dream of. There were those shaped like dragons and great monsters of the deep; candles that swam in water, or appeared to hover in thin air. There were candles in the form of rainbows, where every flame was a different colour, and then there were those crafted with such skill that when you lit them they looked like burning crystal. Candles that played music, or exploded, or smelled of bacon – danced jigs, tasted of marzipan, you name it: that young, noble craftsman made the lot. He could even make candles that burned for a year or more.' Ummond paused for a moment, his eyes fixed wide by the small flame that now wavered above the desk.

'There was something else about that workshop,' he said quietly, almost to himself. A smile flickered briefly like a twitch across his old features. 'It was the only place in the castle from which the Lord could see the girl.' Silence ensued once more. Marcus was about to cough to prompt him, then at the last second for some reason he checked himself. The other's eyes snapped up.

'The land of Ude was covered by dark and dangerous forests,' continued Ummond, breaking into his stride. 'Each Lord or Lady had their own castle and their own servants, and each carried the sole key to their castle's tower. The only way they could see above the tangled trees that covered the earth was by climbing to the very top. Then, using the telescope that each Lord or Lady possessed, they could see into all the other towers of the kingdom where they reached out for the sky. Thus, they always knew what all the other nobles were up to. No one could ever deceive or be deceived; and no one felt alone.

'In the castle across the valley from our candle maker lived a Princess. She was still barely a woman but already her beauty was unsurpassed.'

'Isn't it always?' mumbled Grool.

'You didn't think I'd pick a troll, did you? She and the Lord used to look at each other often through their telescopes, and every night without fail before going to bed, he would leave a candle alight in the workshop that burned until dawn. So it always was and so it had always been.

'When he wasn't busy working upstairs, the Lord attended to matters in the castle. On the first floor were the study, the library and the dining room. Here Grimble, the caretaker, and his Lordship used to sort out the daily running of the household and other business matters, bills and so on, and in the evenings the Lord often had his man standing by for company as he ate. Then, he would sometimes go to the library to read or, if he was in a different sort of humour, he would zip down to the kitchen and share a good old yarn with the cook, Tooley O' Marge.

'Tooley O' Marge was rosy and plump with strawberry blonde hair in a bun and her fingers were rarely not dripping with goose fat or some other lipidinous unction. She was usually the first person visitors would encounter on arrival and she would invite them in with a smile and a laugh and make them welcome by the roaring kitchen fire. She was noisy, big and thoroughly disorganised, and his Lordship would not have parted with Tooley O' Marge for all the gold or candlewax in the kingdom.

'Elbows Mick and Patterson Nitch kept quarters down in the basement. As his name suggests, the castle mason was a strong, fit, active fellow, and it was his task to keep the sound, stone walls and majestic gardens in fine repair. Nitch, in turn, took care of things inside. He was a quiet, unassuming lad and unlike Mick there was barely a scrap to him. You'd never think from looking at them both that they were, in fact, cousins. I forget on whose side now. But don't be fooled: Patterson Nitch worked with the speed and efficiency of twenty men — making the fires, cleaning the chimneys; plumbing, fixing, oiling, stitching, carrying. Without him the entire place would've fallen around their ears and, what's more, he barely ever needed telling. No sooner a job arose that it was done. And so, my boy -'

'What about the other one?' interjected Marcus. 'Fel — Falego?'

'Oh.' The Doctor's face turned sour. 'He was the Spanish imp who fed the beasts. And thus,' he continued, brightening once more, 'the Lord lived happily in his castle and everything ran like clockwork. Every servant knew their task and place, and everyone respected and obeyed his Lordship's command and judgment, for without it their labours would have been wasted. From his tower he made contact with the other nobles of Ude, and he kept his servants regularly informed of all the goings on in the kingdom. And every night, he lit a candle for the Princess across the valley and, sometimes, they would even stay up into the small hours and together stare at the Moon.

'Then, one day, a magician arrived in the land...'

'Mm-m,' said the Lord, dropping his napkin over an empty plate. 'Our Tooley makes the best dumplings in the kingdom. Wouldn't you say, Grimble?'

'Indubitably, Sir,' replied Balthazar Grimble. (Balthazar Grimble was habitually fond of utilising as many superfluous syllables as possible.)

'Take care to thank her again for me.'

'Certainly, Sir.' The caretaker, dressed tidily in a suit and commanding an unbecoming air of dignity, stood some yards from the table as per usual while his Lordship finished his meal. The Lord sat back. Resting a boot up on the chair beside him, he drained his glass of wine.

'Excellent,' he exclaimed. He looked along the length of the inordinate dining table; at the delicate, summer-scented candles shaped as wildflowers that he had finished earlier that day. His eyes narrowed briefly as he appeared to think of something. Then his expression cleared and he sighed a soft smile. 'I must be almost the most contented man alive,' he said aloud.

'I am delivered practically at ecstasy's doorstep to hear

it, Sir,' the caretaker responded.

'Are you content, Grimble?' the Lord asked suddenly. He turned his young head with its wavy locks of gold towards the other. 'You don't always appear so, you know?'

Grimble raised his eyebrows, somewhat surprised at the unusual nature of his master's question. He laughed bashfully. 'But your Lordship, I exist in a state beyond contentment simply by being in your service.'

'Really?' returned the other, thinking. Then he fixed the servant with a look that contained genuine intrigue, and also a playful touch of sport. 'So there's nothing you desire above what you have now?'

'Categorically in the negative, M' Lord,' answered Grimble, flustering slightly. The two men regarded one another. A great grin broke over his Lordship's face. He let the matter drop.

'I am extremely pleased to hear it, my loyal Grimble.' The caretaker inclined a small bow. 'Be a good fellow, would you, and nip down and ask Tooley if she'd make me some coffee? I'll be in the library.' The young man rose and stretched with a satisfied yelp before striding his quick form next door to where a fire was blazing.

'Certainly, Sir.' With his usual, measured manner, Grimble started to clear the table. His mind, however, had already begun to race.

* * *

'Ah. Thank you very much, Grimble.'

'Sir. Might his Lordship require anything else?'

'No, thank you. That'll be all for this evening.' Balthazar Grimble nodded. Hesitating for a moment and fidgeting slightly, he said, more abruptly than intended:

'Your Lordship, there was actually one thing that occurred to me – oh, do forgive me, Sir.'

'No, that's all right,' said the Lord looking up from his book. At his feet, Hamlet, the old Great Dane, yawned contentedly. 'Tell me.'

'Well…' The caretaker scrunched at his knuckles, as he did when he was agitated. 'Well, Sir,' he said, clearing his throat. 'It's regarding the sealed section of the bookcase in the corner there.'

Both men looked over. The end of the bookcase was locked securely behind a cupboard door that bore the family's crest.

'I am most grateful, naturally,' continued Grimble hastily, 'for his Lordship's generous permission to peruse so many wonderful volumes as it is, but it is on occasion that I find myself wondering what manner of tome his Lordship might keep in such secrecy.' He gave a high little nervous laugh and traced a finger over his creased brow.

The Lord regarded his servant with a knowing smile.

'All books are not written for all men,' said the Lord. 'You'll just have to trust me on that, my good Grimble.'

'Yes, but if his Lordship will pardon my lack of temerity, how might one come to increase one's knowledge if one does not have access to all the knowledge available?'

The young noble chuckled softly and settled back once more in his armchair. 'Knowledge without understanding is an extremely dangerous thing, Grimble,' he replied. 'And understanding does not begin with books. In the wrong hands, the contents of that cupboard there could do untold damage and harm.'

'And where, Sir,' asked the caretaker dryly, 'does one learn about understanding, if not from books?'

The Lord entertained a soft, private smile. 'If you really want the answer to that,' he said, 'you should go and have a chat with Tooley O' Marge.'

The caretaker paused. Then, swallowing, he said, 'Thank you, Sir. Will that be all?'

'Yes thank you, Grimble. Good night.'

'Good night, Sir.'

Unseen by his Lordship, Balthazar Grimble's face as he closed the library doors behind him was that of a blowfish pickled in vinegar.

*   *   *

The following morning, the Lord went downstairs bright and early as usual to the kitchen for breakfast. It was a great, homely room and it looked, as ever, as though an earthquake had just hit. Patterson Nitch already had the fire blazing and he nodded nervously to his Lordship as the latter entered the room. He seated himself casually at the gnarled, old wooden table. 'Morning, Tooley,' he called cheerfully.

The mobile hillock, if not quite mountain, that was the young Tooley O' Marge turned redly about. 'Oh, bless me,' she exclaimed. 'I didn't hear your Lordship come in. And a good morning to you n' all, Sir.'

'Any chance of some bacon and eggs?'

'Just as give me one minute there...' She removed her sticky hands from the immense mixing bowl in which they had been immersed and, wiping them on her filthy apron, went to the larder.

('Is there electricity?' Marcus Grool asked suddenly.

'What what?'

The other man shuffled. 'I just wondered if the castle had electricity.'

'Oh, I see,' said Ummond. 'A details man, eh? Very well, Grool, it's your bankruptcy. What d' ya see?'

Marcus thought. He imagined Tooley O' Marge with an electric whisk; Patterson Nitch adjusting the TV; and a radio blaring in

50

the background. He turned his nose up. 'No, I – I don't think so,'
he said.

The Doctor curled a smile. 'A traditionalist after all. Then spit and
polish it shall be. O' Marge came out of the larder and placed a frying
pan over the fire. . .')

'Wonderful dumplings last night,' said the Lord with a wink.

Tooley blushed. 'Mr Grimble told me your Lordship liked 'em,' she said coyly. The bacon hissed loudly into the pan. 'I know they're your Lordship's favourite. I only makes 'em for you, Sir – and meself, of course. Mr Grimble turns his nose up at 'em and, well, Elbows Mick loves 'em but he reckons too many'll turn him fat. I ask you: when did a couple of dumplings ever make anybody fat?' She waddled over to the big stone basin and drew water into the kettle. The Lord smiled. Then his face became serious.

'Tooley: I wanted to ask you something.'

'Yes, your Lordship?' She returned to the fire and hung the kettle in the hearth. She cracked a couple of eggs.

'I received a signal from the Duke yesterday,' the young man continued. He pinched salt between his fingers and let it fall idly. 'Apparently there's a magician arrived in the kingdom. One Seer Fanta.'

'A magician? Well well.' Tooley flipped the bacon on its back.

'He's calling all the Lords of the land together to go on a journey across the sea.' His Lordship brushed his fingertips together and sat back. 'According to what he told the Duke there's a long lost island out towards the World's End. It's inhabited by an ancient race of peoples who are supposed to possess riches beyond compare. And, as this Seer Fanta fellow would have it, he has the only existing charts of how to get there.' The Lord fell quiet. Tooley made no immediate reply, but served him up his breakfast. When back at the sink, she said:

'Is his Grace going, then?'

'Uh-hm,' said the other through a too-hot mouthful. Patterson Nitch excused himself and disappeared to other chores. 'The Duke's going. Everyone is. There's talk that even the King himself is considering it.'

'I see,' said Tooley. She scrubbed vigorously at the heavy frying pan with a wire brush. 'Well, then. If everyone's off on this magical jamboree, your Lordship won't want to miss out, will he?'

'That's what I wanted to ask you,' said the Lord, looking over at the cook's round back. He rested his knife and fork. 'Tooley: look at me.' She turned. 'What do you think? Honestly?'

'Honestly?' He nodded. 'Honestly, I think you've got all the riches you need right here and you know it,' she replied, sighing her great frame against the sink. 'Not to mention,' she added, 'a certain young lady in the castle across the valley who I've heard so much speak of. How long's this great adventure s'posed to last anyway?'

The Lord shrugged. 'I don't know,' he said, resuming his breakfast. 'A year? Two? Mm, this is delicious.'

'She'll be a woman soon,' said the other, a note of warning in her voice.

'Yup,' agreed the Lord. He sucked in the last, jelly-white piece of fried egg. 'But a young man must have adventures. You know that, don't you? Before he becomes old and dry and decrepit.' He hunched his back and twisted up his face in a toothless snarl. Tooley O' Marge shook her head, then began to chuckle merrily.

'Oh, you'll do as you do, Sir. You always do that. Here: what's Mr Grimble said about all this, then?'

The other straightened. 'I haven't mentioned it yet, actually,' he said. 'Thought I'd just test where the water's hottest first.'

Tooley took a deep breath. 'We'll all miss your Lordship,' she said. 'But if adventure it must be — well: you go to it, Sir.'

'Thank you, Tooley,' he said fondly. 'And don't you worry about the Princess. I've a plan.'

* * *

At dinner that evening, the Lord was unusually quiet as he ate. After dessert had been cleared, Balthazar Grimble at last summoned his courage and, coughing gently, asked: 'Would his Lordship object if I posed a question?' The other waved him on. 'I happened to hear earlier,' continued Grimble, 'that a certain magician was in the land and that a voyage to a very distant island was currently in preparation. Had his Lordship heard of this?'

'Indeed I had,' replied the Lord. 'How did you hear of it?'

Grimble looked to his shiny shoes. 'Well, I, er... Patterson Nitch, actually, M' Lord. I noted Mr Nitch looking, shall we say, peculiarly anxious earlier, Sir, and after gentle probing he furnished me with the information.' The caretaker smiled weakly.

'Very well,' said the Lord. He added nothing further.

'Ahem. I did wonder,' pressed Grimble, 'what might be his Lordship's intentions regarding the enterprise. I was thinking solely of practical considerations in the event of a continued absence, if M' Lord understands my meaning,' the caretaker concluded.

The Lord looked at his servant for some time. He scratched his chin. 'Would you go?' he asked at length.

'I? Why, I...' The other stammered, unused as he was to being asked his own, personal opinion. 'I think I would... well, that is-'

'Have a seat, Grimble,' said the Lord. He pushed the chair adjacent to him back from the table. 'Come on. We never really talk – properly. As men should.' Grimble moved nervously, and with much scrunching of knuckles, to where he was now directed. Ever so slowly, glancing often towards his master for assurance, he lowered his skinny bottom down onto the chair. He forced a smile. 'There,' said the Lord. 'That wasn't so bad. Here: have some wine.' His Lordship reached for a glass and poured.

The caretaker regarded the dining room about him as though viewing it for the first time. It occurred to him that the last person to have sat where he was sitting now was none other than his Lordship's best friend, the Duke himself. He felt a small sense of thrill run through him.

'I can never quite work you out,' said the Lord.

'Sir?'

'Quite what you're made of, Grimble.' He stared at the caretaker with piercing eyes. 'You're efficient, quick-witted; good with the accounts.'

'Oh, really your Lordship. Really?' Grimble began to glow.

'Even known to tell a story or two. And, of course,' added the Lord, reaching for his glass, 'I can trust you to organise the others. But what I want to know, Grimble, now that it's just you and I talking, is what would you do?'

'Do, Sir?'

'Yes: *do*. If the choice were yours to make. Would you risk it all on a mad adventure, with the possibility that you might just make a difference somewhere – or does one simply accept what one already has, to live always knowing that maybe you never really tried?' There was a long pause while the caretaker considered. The Lord drank as he did so, watching. 'Just think,' he said quietly at last. 'Beyond the sea. Knowledge, Grimble. Knowledge, and books – riches.' He trailed off and his eyes narrowed. 'People to help...'

'I couldn't go, Sir,' blurted the young caretaker suddenly. His master sat back in surprise. 'I'm just not brave enough, I'm afraid that's the veracity of the situation. Books and theories are fine but – the sea is wet, your Lordship!'

The other blinked. 'I know it is, Grimble.'

'And deep.'

'Deeper than a man, in places.'

'And there could be pirates, or tidal waves, or' – Grimble blenched – 'extremely savage fish... Oh, Sir! The thought is too much to bear!'

The Lord leaned forward and patted the other man's shoulder. Inwardly, he smiled a fond smile. 'I know,' he said. Then he drew in a deep breath and sighed. 'So what do I do, eh?' he asked, half to himself. 'Do I go? Or is it just a foolish quest?'

His servant looked to him pleadingly. 'I didn't mean to sound alarmist, your Lordship.' He began to regain his composure. 'I know a young Lord must do as he does. But if you were to leave, Sir, I should fear for the castle's safety. I can organise all the day to day affairs by myself, naturally, but the important decisions, I…' He raised his palms feebly.

'You think I should stay?' said the Lord gravely at length.

'I think his Lordship should first inspect this magician's credentials,' Grimble replied.

The Lord thought. 'A good idea, Grimble,' he acknowledged, rising. 'No, no – you sit there and finish your wine. I will contact the Duke, and in the morning you and I shall compose a telegram inviting the magician to call on us. See what this Seer Fanta's made of, eh? Night night.'

'Good, er – yes: goodnight, Sir.' The caretaker was left alone in the dining room. He looked at the glass in his hand. The prospect of his master leaving the castle truly gave him a sensation of butterflies, and many other, less pleasant insects, in the pit of his stomach. His Lordship had never deserted them for any considerable period of time before. The idea was terrifying. And yet, mused Grimble, running his hand along the table top as a tiny light flickered on in his mind… He turned to look at the Lord's empty chair. '*Your Grace* – Good evening, my Lord. May I give you some advice?'

The Lord unlocked the sturdy, oak door and closed it again behind him. He ran lightly up the narrow, spiral staircase. Upstairs, the workshop was grey and shapeless in the waning evening light. He paused to light a gas lamp by the stairwell and suddenly the entire room filled with vibrant colours. Candles in various stages of design or completion lay absolutely everywhere in their thousands. Selecting one from a rack on the wall, he took it quickly over to the window.

In the tower across the valley, the Princess was already watching for him. The Lord looked at her through his telescope and smiled. In the flicker of golden oil light, she was young and mysterious and true. He waved and she waved back to him. Then he set the candle he had chosen in a special candlestick by the window and, lighting it, returned to his workbench and his tools. The night was not long. And on this particular night, he had two most exceptional candles to make indeed.

*   *   *

Seer Fanta was everything you might expect of an infamous, wandering magician. He had shining, black eyes set in a dark face with a thin moustache and he wore robes that were embroidered with the Sun and the Moon. He was short and quite round, and on his feet he wore shoes whose toes curled right back upon themselves. His nose was the hook of an eagle's beak and he had a smile like a scimitar. He spoke a strange, guttural language the Lord had never heard before, and the two men conversed through an interpreter — a shifty-looking fellow — for almost an hour as they walked about the herb garden.

At the upstairs library window, Balthazar Grimble watched surreptitiously from behind a curtain. From where he stood, the Seer and his brightly sequinned entourage looked quite the most exciting and intriguing band of travellers he had ever seen. Downstairs in the kitchen, however, Tooley O' Marge saw nothing but an untrustworthy rabble of mountebanks and jugglers. She watched through narrow, worried eyes as her fat hands automatically washed and squeezed the linen. Nitch, as usual, saw nothing of what was going on, so busy was he with his chores. His cousin Elbows Mick glanced over occasionally from where he was clipping the topiary, but thought neither one way nor the other about it. As for Falego…

'What do you think you're doing in here?' shouted Tooley, wheeling suddenly at the squeal of terror that had emanated from the kitchen cat. The young Spanish boy released the poor creature's tail, the underside of which he had been inspecting with unseemly fascination. Beneath the tremulous glare of the cook, Falego hopped up off bare knees and walked nonchalantly outside. Tooley went after him to the door. 'And don't you come back,' she called, slamming it shut. She returned to the laundry. 'I know your sort, my lad,' she muttered.

Eventually, smiling and bowing profusely, the Seer and his mob departed and the Lord came inside. There was an aura of nervous anticipation below his typically cheerful, relaxed demeanour. 'Well, Tooley,' he said to her anxious expression. 'I'm going. The Brave Seadreamer sails with the tide. Even the King is coming with us.' Master and servant regarded one another for a moment. Then Tooley, swallowing a tear, said:

'Very good, your Lordship. I'll help you pack,' and turned away.

Just over an hour later, all five servants convened on the carriage sweep before the castle. The Duke and several other Lords had gathered there also on their way to the harbour, and now their steeds whinnied impatiently at the wait and rolled their eyes. His Lordship himself looked dashing in his travelling cloak and breastplate, his sword ready at his side. He swung up into the saddle and looked down at his loyal retainers.

'Look after one another, now,' he said, regarding them fondly. Each nodded solemnly. 'I'll be back before you know it.' He reined his horse around to depart. At the last moment, he held back once more. He beckoned over to Tooley O' Marge, who came uncertainly forward.

'Sir?'

'I want you to take care of this for me,' the Lord whispered. He held something heavy out to her, wrapped in tissue paper. Frowning, she took it. 'In the tower,' the Lord continued in a hushed but steady voice, 'a candle is burning. I shall return before it dies. If I do not...' He kept the other's gaze. 'You understand.'

'Yes, Sir,' said Tooley, holding herself.

'Good. Thank you, Tooley.' He smiled warmly at her.

'And this, Sir?' She balanced the curious parcel in her hand.

'That, we shall have on my return when we are all together again,' replied the Lord. Then he added: 'With dumplings.'

'Yes, Sir,' repeated the cook unhappily. 'Sir, pardon my boldness, but must you really go? What do you need from some funny old folk in a land you've never seen?'

Behind them, the Duke's horse tossed its mane and snorted loudly. The Lord signalled he was almost done. 'Why,' he said, returning to Tooley with a strange smile on his face, 'I don't need anything.' And saying thus, he carefully pulled open his saddlebag, just enough so that only Tooley could see. As she peered into the deep, leather container, the cook had to stifle a gasp. The saddlebag was stuffed to bursting with hundreds of wonderful candles. Looking her in the eye, the Lord leaned down from his saddle. 'Everyone needs a light to follow,' he whispered, and tapped his nose. Then, with a wink, he gave a great cheer and wheeled about. His mount reared up and whinnied loudly as the other riders cheered with him. Seconds later, he and his fellow Lords had disappeared in a thundering crash of hooves.

The brave young nobles rode out into the valley, across the shallow river and up into the woods on the other side. As they passed a turning in the trail, the Lord fell silent and cast a wistful eye in the direction of what he knew was the Princess' castle.

The Duke saw his companion's gaze and smiled. He leaned across. 'Are you afraid she won't wait for you?' he asked.

The Lord broke from his reverie. 'No.' He shook his head, then smiled back at his friend. 'No, I'm not afraid of that.'

'And how might that be?' the Duke enquired, one eyebrow raised.

'Because,' replied the Lord, 'the part in us that is occupied by hunting, sports and war, in women consists of patience. Ours generally ends when theirs does.'

The Duke contemplated and then, with a playful look, said: 'Ah – but which is the more virtuous?'

'I'm sorry?'

'Which has the greater virtue: patience, or hunting, sports and war?'

The Lord smiled. 'I don't understand the question,' he replied. 'Isn't it all the same thing?' The two young men regarded one another. Then they laughed warmly.

Not long after, the group of horsemen crested the brow of a hill. As the trees parted before them, the great ocean came into view. Down on the jetty, her sails ready unfurled, lay the ship The Brave Seadreamer.

The noblemen drew up for a moment and looked at one another. Then, with an enormous "Hie!" they all galloped on madly down to the shore. The breeze was fair and the Sun shone brightly as the Lords rode merrily on to their destiny. A cry from the ship's bows signalled away with the anchor and, without so much as a look back towards their homeland, they sailed out over the glassy sea.

5

THAT'S IT.'

'Hm?'

'Your time's up.' Ummond leaned forward and batted out the flame with his hand.

Blinking, Marcus Grool snapped as if from a trance and looked at the candle. It had, indeed, burned itself quietly down to the figure "II". Outside, it was getting dark.

'So,' said the Doctor, stretching with a crack of bones. 'Do you want to write me the cheque now? Or shall we exorcise a little cliché and say "Same time next week"?'

'Next week?' Marcus composed himself. 'Yes. Next week is fine.'

'Let's hope so,' said the Doctor quietly with a particular smile.

*　*　*

That evening, Marcus walked back along the street where he lived with an uncommon sense of calm. He looked up at a streetlight and for the first time in his memory wondered how life must have been when someone had to come and light each individual gas lamp every night. Naturally, he thought, once more back on track, the Doctor was still a lunatic, and he saw no connection between the story and his own predicament. But he had to hand it to the old man: he did have a way of telling a...a what was it? A "yarn".

He'd have to do the whole ten hours, of course. He wasn't going to pay £10 000 for a story, however well told. But then that also worked. For a start, it would keep him occupied for an afternoon a week while he was job-hunting – entertained, even, although Ummond's personal jibes still irked him. Yes, he might have to mention that next time. Equally, though, it would keep Elizabeth happy. Marcus allowed himself a smile. He had planned it perfectly once again.

'You went back to see Dr Ummond, then?' said Elizabeth later when the television had been switched off.

'Yes, well, I thought I'd give him another chance. You know.'

Elizabeth playfully pinched her boyfriend's cheeks. 'Who's a big, brave boy?' she said, and went to boil the kettle.

'Zooks! Grool – you again. You're becoming some kind of regular here.'

Marcus acknowledged with a quick smile and sat himself down.

A week had passed, yet the Doctor appeared to have made little progress with the pocket watch. The desk was a dull graveyard of tiny cogs and wheels. Many of them were rusted. Dr Ummond squinted through a jeweller's magnifying glass, which he had plugged against one eye. At last, he gave up. 'Blasted thing. Oh well,' he said, sweeping the pieces away once more and lighting the candle on the desk between them.

'Why don't you take it to the watchmaker over there?' asked Marcus.

The Doctor grimaced. 'You may find, my lad,' he replied, feeling absently for the top of his dandelion hairdo, 'that as you get older there is a certain satisfaction to be gained from doing things yourself. All right? Now: where were we?'

'Doctor?' put in Marcus before the other could begin.

Ummond frowned. 'You what?'

'I just said "Doctor",' repeated Marcus, muddled.

'Oh. What d' ya say that for?'

The other shifted. 'Because that's your profession. Isn't it?' He pointed to a card on the desk. Ummond stared. He waved a hand.

'Don't go believing everything you read,' he said dismissively.

'But-'

'Look, laddie.' The old man leaned across. His eyes narrowed. 'I put that on the card so as sick people like yourself might take me seriously,' he said, emphasising the last word. 'For what I do, there aren't any generally recognised qualifications, ya see?' He sat back. 'It's a bit like calling yourself a banker when you phone to make an appointment instead of "Can't shovel together two farthings with a fork-lift truck" unemployed. Know what I mean?' An eyebrow arched.

'I may have an interview this week,' said Marcus, shuffling embarrassedly. He felt peculiarly transparent.

Ummond continued. 'Call me what you like, doesn't make any difference to me. Except "sugar". Patient who was a boxer, once. Seven foot African-American fellow – kept calling me "sugar". Made me lose the thread completely... What was it you wanted?'

'The present,' replied the younger man, clearing his throat. 'That the Lord gave to the cook before he left. You didn't say what it was.'

'Ahh…the present.' The Doctor, as Marcus saw him, regarded his patient with just the smallest flicker of approval. 'That was well remembered, Grool.' He smacked the desk. 'Now keep your ears sharp. A week after the Lord's departure, Tooley O' Marge, out of a hitherto dormant sense of curiosity, decided to go upstairs and do a spot of cleaning. In the library she found the dog, Hamlet, lying on the floor beside Grimble, who was sat reading a book in his Lordship's chair with his feet up before the fire…'

'Balthazar,' reprimanded the cook severely. 'I thought that were his Lordship's chair. What are you doing sitting in it?'

The caretaker's forehead creased in condescension. 'I am cogitating upon the words of a masterful scribe,' he said without looking up. He licked a dry finger and turned a page.

Tooley dusted over a side table. 'Well, I don't care what you call it,' she said with disapproval. 'You shouldn't be doing it in the master's chair.' As though in agreement, Hamlet yawned with a whine. 'What if you're seen?' she added, shaking the rag.

'Do you mind?' remarked Grimble. 'I am endeavouring to concentrate. And as for being observed, it does not concern me. No doubt his Lordship shall be absent for some time.'

'Got a letter from him today, matter of fact,' said Tooley, ceasing her dusting. She produced the letter from where it had been safely concealed in her enormous bosom. 'It says that he hopes we's all well and that the castle's still standing; that they've been going from port to port collecting young nobles from all over; and that he's fed up with fish and stale water and'd do anything to taste a dumpling right now. Ah, bless.' Smiling, she replaced the letter in its stronghold. Then, her face fell stern. 'And I don't care if his Lordship don't see you with his own eyes, Balthazar Grimble, 'cause I seen you and I'll tell him meself when he gets back, d' you hear?'

The caretaker did not deign to look up. 'No doubt you will,' he said haughtily. 'Now have you quite finished? I thought you belonged downstairs.'

Tooley shot him a furious glance. 'Somebody's got to keep this place tidy while you're loafing about.' With a huff, she clumped her way to the door.

'Oh, and one other thing, Miss Marge,' called Grimble. 'From now on I think it would be more appropriate if you were to address me as "Mr Grimble", if you don't mind. Just so there's no misunderstanding. After all,' he said, inhaling grandly, 'I am the Major Domo now.'

Tooley glared from the hallway. 'You're a major something, all right, Balthazar Grimble,' she said narrowly, 'but I wouldn't want to say what in front of the dog.' With that, she stormed off.

The caretaker stared for a moment at the space where she had been. Then he returned to his reading. 'Unruly old barge,' he muttered to himself. Suddenly, he let out a shrill laugh. 'Unruly old barge,' he repeated, tittering. Beside him, Hamlet barked. 'Shut up,' snapped Grimble.

This was just the beginning.

The following day, there was a knock at the kitchen door. Tooley, picking sticky balls of unbaked dough from between her chubby fingers, bustled over to open it. Two dour-looking faces she did not recognise stared back at her. 'Morning?' she said uncertainly.

'We are here to call upon Mr Grimble,' the female of the pair said brusquely. She pushed a pair of spectacles back up her long nose. 'This is my companion Mr Fusset and I am Ms Fawcett. How do you do?' She and Mr Fusset extended their hands peremptorily in unison. Tooley shook them. 'May we come in?' asked Ms Fawcett in her piercing voice.

'May you..? Well, yes,' replied Tooley, standing aside in somewhat of a daze. Checking outside for anything else unusual, she closed the door. 'Can I offer you something? Cup of tea? Kettle's just boiled.'

'Uh, no, thank you,' said Mr Fusset with an exaggerated smile. He too wore glasses, and a bowler hat. They were both dressed impeccably. 'We have several delicate matters to discuss with Mr Grimble, and we rather-'

'A-huh,' coughed Ms Fawcett with a sharp glance at her fellow visitor.

'Oh, yes. Of course.' They both smiled quickly. A ponderous silence ensued as they continued to all stand there in the kitchen. The fire crackled away in the background.

'Well,' announced Tooley at last, rubbing her hands together. 'Will you be staying for lunch, then?' However, before either visitor could answer, Balthazar Grimble swept grandly into the room.

'Ah, my dear friends — forgive me. Mr Fusset, Ms Fawcett, what a joy to have you here. Please, please, come upstairs at once. I must apologise for the deplorable state of these surroundings.' He cast a scornful eye at Tooley and her beloved kitchen. 'I assure you, you will be far more comfortable in the library,' and he ushered them out before they could so much as draw another breath.

Tooley tapped her foot on the flagstones and crossed her strong arms. 'You'd best watch out, Balthazar Grimble,' she said across the empty room. 'I know you're up to something. I can tell these things.'

The following day, two more people arrived. The day after that, three. It soon became apparent to Tooley and the other servants that these "visitors" were in no hurry to leave. After a fortnight had passed, the first floor of the castle was filled to bursting with these mysterious new characters. The poor cook worked day and night trying to feed them all and, what did not make life any easier, was that they all had different requirements. Some ate meat, others no green vegetables; some liked only sweet foods, some only dishes that had not been cooked, and so on. She had to enlist the aid of Elbows Mick to supply and carry all the food, and the pair were soon exhausted. Tooley wished she had some way of contacting his Lordship; but the ship was ever moving from port to port and, though she continued to receive his letters, she could not reply.

Then, one day, Mick strode into the kitchen in a foul temper. Rolling down his overalls from his solid chest and arms, he marched over to the shelf where the cider was kept and unstopped himself a jar. He tipped his head back and poured a long draught down his throat.

'Bit early in the day for festivities, innit?' said Tooley, looking up from the fireplace. She was sweating over a gigantic cauldron and assorted pots and pans, as almost always these days. The kitchen was even messier than usual.

Elbows Mick wiped his mouth. He looked at her seriously. 'I don't know what this place is coming to, Miss Tooley,' he said, shaking his head. He took another swig of cider.

'Oh, so you've noticed and all,' returned Tooley gravely.

'I was just up at the top cleaning windows,' continued Mick, 'when that Fawcett woman sticks her head out and says she's decided she wants the castle roof painted bright pink. It's the fashion, she squawks. Well, I say, that's all very well, but it's Mr Grimble on behalf of his Lordship who usually tells me what needs fixing. She gives me a look that I don't care to describe, then five minutes later comes back with Mr Grimble himself. Is this right then, Mr Grimble, I say, about the roof being painted pink? He looks at me, right, and then in a tone of voice he's never used with me before, he says: "Of course it is, you great loaf. Don't question Ms Fawcett again" – and slams the window shut! Well, I ask you: what would his Lordship think? A pink roof? Don't see anything wrong with the original, far as I'm concerned.' He swallowed another gulp and replaced the jar. 'They'll be telling me to enlarge the turrets next.'

At that moment, Patterson Nitch entered the room. He was even more frantic than usual. 'Hello, Patterson,' said Tooley warmly. 'Can I get you anything?'

'Oh, n-no thank you, Miss T-Tooley,' he stammered with a quick, thin smile. His face was pale and nervous.

'You all right, Pat?' asked his cousin with concern.

'Yeah,' added Tooley. 'You don't 'alf look queer.'

Nitch wrung his hands. 'Really, just p-passing,' he replied meekly. 'All these visitors are p-playing havoc with the p-pipes, that's all. Must fly,' and he was off through the other door down to the basement muttering something about rising pressure.

Tooley shook her head and raised her eyes suspiciously at the ceiling. 'What are they up to up there?' she said.

Later that day, she could bear the mystery no longer. Having crept upstairs as quietly as she was able, Tooley heard voices coming from beyond in the library. She opened one of the doors a sliver and peeked inside. There, over in the far corner, she beheld a most peculiar sight.

Surrounded by a dozen or so of his strange, new acquaintances, Balthazar Grimble stood before the locked section of the bookcase doing an extraordinary thing. As Tooley watched, she saw the caretaker raise his hands, close his eyes and, muttering some unintelligible gibberish, wave his arms at the sealed door. When nothing happened, he collapsed feebly and all the visitors crowded about to confer heatedly before he tried again. After she had watched him fail for the third time in this unfathomable endeavour, Tooley could bear it no longer.

'Balthazar Grimble what on Earth do you think you're playing at?' the cook fired at him as she stormed in. Startled, all present jumped in fright and parted cowardly at the crimson giant's approach.

'What are you doing in here?' demanded Grimble, backing away. 'This is my library.' Tooley continued to advance until, finally, she had the helpless caretaker pinned against the wall by her heaving bosom.

'This,' she said fiercely, 'is his Lordship's library and his Lordship's castle, and as one of his Lordship's servants I demand to know what is going on in it. And if,' she finished, 'you don't tell me straight away then I'm gonna breathe in until I hear your head go pop. D' you understand?'

Grimble's eyes flitted down to where his nose was already squashed uncomfortably to one side. He nodded quickly. 'Good,' said the cook. Satisfied, she backed up and let the other drop. She waited.

'That cupboard,' said Grimble, panting somewhat, 'contains some exceedingly rare and most special books. If we can access them, our intelligence and knowledge will soar. This castle,' he declared, straightening, 'will become the cleverest and most knowledgeable establishment in the whole of the land. We will be recognised, admired –

worshipped by all. We shall be the toast of the kingdom. We' – he paused dramatically – 'shall be kings!' There was a ripple of applause from the visitors.

'Them books,' Tooley said firmly, 'are for his Lordship. And we was doing perfectly well the way we was before, thank you very much. So don't go talking to me about your "intelligence". I know what's what.'

'His Lordship's gone,' moaned Grimble pathetically. 'We need all the help we can get.'

Tooley regarded him. The caretaker's face pleaded feebly. She scanned across the other silent, tight visages in the room. At last, she flapped a big arm. 'Well. I won't say you haven't got a point. But I don't want nothing to do with it, you understand? I'll just pretend I ain't seen nothing.' With a nod, she turned and started to walk towards the door. 'You'll have to open it first, anyway,' she called back over her shoulder.

Behind her, Grimble's mouth twisted. 'We'll get it open,' he said, eyes hungry like a serpent's. 'Seer Fanta's coming to open it personally.'

Tooley span around. 'What? But he went with the Lords.'

The caretaker shook his head. 'He exchanged the charts for a share of the treasure when they return. I received a telegram from him only last week. He promised to visit us soon, to help us in our time of need. And you,' he said, waving a long, slim finger, 'will let him in and be courteous, O' Marge, when he arrives. You may think you know what goes on around here but you don't, understand? You're just the cook. Now go back to your sink where you belong. And remember' – Grimble's eyes gleamed wickedly – 'there's more of us than there is of even you.'

Downstairs, Tooley O' Marge's heart beat in a flutter. It was too much to bear. Seer Fanta – here again? With his gangly hangers-on and that oily interpreter... A shiver like ice-cold water ran down her spine. Banging the door aside, she hurried into the kitchen larder and pulled open a drawer.

Inside, still carefully wrapped in its tissue paper, was the parcel his Lordship had handed her on the day he had left. Looking at it now, it seemed to Tooley as though an age had since passed. She took the parcel out and opened it slowly. The paper fell away to reveal a candle – the second he had made on his last night in the castle. It was thick and brightly coloured, and decorated in extravagant, slightly gaudy spirals and whirls. Tooley re-wrapped it and then closed the empty drawer. 'We'd best put you somewhere safe,' she said. Sadly she added: 'Nothing's going to be safe when that Seer Fanta arrives. Nothing.'

* * *

The magician did indeed arrive, the very next afternoon. Smiling oleaginously with his glittering black eyes, he made his way through the kitchen and headed straight upstairs with his troop. Tooley said nothing, but slammed the door after them with a thud.

In the library, the newcomers were received with great excitement. Grimble, standing theatrically aside, presented the locked bookcase and bowed. Muttering in that peculiar language of his, the magician eyed it up and frowned. He took a deep breath. He closed his eyes. He raised his hands. A second later, and with a great, bellowing cry, he lifted his right leg and, using all his force, planted his heel through the door lock. The wood splintered and shattered. Ever so slowly, the door swung open on its hinges to reveal row after row of beautiful, leather bound books.

Everyone stared and paused. A moment later, a great cheer erupted from the visitors and eager hands were thrust inside. Grimble, beaming, approached the magician, who was smiling tirelessly beneath his accolade.

'Stupendous, your — your magicalness,' the caretaker gushed. 'Simply…stupendous.' Seer Fanta raised his hands in disingenuous humility, then babbled something to his interpreter.

'My master asks if he may take some of the other books from the library as payment for his hermetic unsealing,' the interpreter said.

Grimble clasped his hands together in ecstasy. 'Anything you want,' he sighed. 'Take anything. You're welcome!'

Tooley heard no more goings on above for some days. She, together with Nitch and Elbows Mick, had no time to stop, however. With over a dozen mouths to feed before counting their own, they worked day and night until they were almost exhausted. Patterson Nitch grew thinner and more jittery than ever, and Mick began to drain cider at an alarming rate. The guttering on the castle walls became blocked but the mason had either no time or no inclination to clear it. As a result, everything began to smell of damp and was very cheerless indeed.

As for Tooley, she could barely even think straight any more. Her hands were raw with work and her back began to pain her. She had half a mind to just give in there and then and resign. However, the thought of abandoning the place where she had spent her life, and most of it contentedly, fortunately for all concerned made her stay. As long as she was there, there was a chance that things could be put straight, she told herself. There was always a way.

For Falego's part, he continued quietly to feed the animals in their pen at the far end of the garden. The young

Spanish boy observed all, but for the most part kept hidden in his alcove in the basement. His time would come. And besides, he was still growing.

One day, as the sky brought in the first chill wind to dampen the long-grass beyond the garden, and the leaves of the forest surrounding the castle were beginning to turn, there was something like an explosion and the kitchen door through to the upstairs stairway flew open. There, dressed entirely in black from head to foot, with a cane, top hat and heavy, velvet cloak, stood Balthazar Grimble. He surveyed the scene of endless labour before him from along the end of his nose. Then, with a twirl of his cane, he swept majestically into the kitchen. His acquaintances, similarly attired, followed quickly behind. The caretaker glanced imperiously about once more. Without regarding Tooley, he declared: 'We are commandeering this kitchen.'

Tooley O' Marge stared at them in disbelief. She caught sight of Seer Fanta hovering in the doorway. She dropped her work and scowled. 'Oh no you're not.'

There was a tense moment's hesitation. At a gesture from Grimble, the visitors dispersed about the kitchen and larder and began rifling across the work surfaces, among the shelves and through drawers. Tooley seemed as though she might burst any second. Her face glowed hot as a radish.

'Balthazar Grimble! What is the meaning of this?'

The caretaker studied a fingernail. 'It has become evident,' he sniffed, 'from the insufficient diet we have of late endured – not to mention the deplorable state of this kitchen – that you are incapable of fulfilling even your rudimentary function on these premises.' Tooley started to protest but Grimble hushed her by lifting a china jug on the end of his ebony cane. He dangled it threateningly above the stone floor. 'We shall therefore be taking charge in here from now on,' he said and, for emphasis, he let the jug fall. It shattered into tiny blue pieces. Before Tooley could respond, he had lifted another.

'I'm warning you, Balthazar,' growled the cook. The caretaker merely raised his eyebrows and let the second jug smash before selecting a third. The two circled one another. 'You've lost your conkers!' cried Tooley. 'We'll all starve. What do you know about cooking, anyway?'

Grimble turned on her. 'I,' he snarled, 'know about everything.' The visitors ceased in their tampering to watch as their chairman ascended the kitchen table. 'I have more knowledge than you can possibly imagine. I have read the Cabala,' he began, staring intensely; 'I have read the Talmud and the Tarot. I have studied and assimilated the works of Confucius, Zoroaster and Plato and single-handedly defined the inscriptions on the Emerald Tablet of the great

Hermes Trismegistus. I have read Shakespeare,' he went on, working into a frenzy, 'devoured Descartes, Mallory and Fraser – exposed the amateur ramblings of Schopenhauer, Nietzsche and Freud; I have intoned the sacred "Om" and recovered the lost New Testament Gospels; answered the eternal hexagram – solved the riddle of the knights Templar. I have located the Grail, the head of Christ, resolved the anomalies of astrophysics, found the elixir of life, and I have deciphered the secret universal code in the House at Pooh Corner!' There was a fervent roar of approval from the visitors.

'Bravo! Bravo!' clapped Ms Fawcett.

'Indomitable, Sir!' cried Fusset. 'Indomitable!'

'We shall perform alchemy!'

Seer Fanta watched smiling from the corner. He stroked his moustache.

'Is that right?' shouted Tooley O' Marge. The room fell nervously quiet once more. She glared at Balthazar Grimble. Slowly, she said: 'Make me a dumpling.'

The caretaker leaned down with a nefarious smile. 'My good woman,' he replied softly. 'You already are one. Now get out!'

Outside on the gravel, Tooley wept warm, fat tears. She turned her face up to the tower where the Lord's candle shone, faint but sure in the daylight. 'Please come back, Sir,' she implored it quietly. 'Oh please come home.'

From the rooftop, Elbows Mick watched her. He took another long pull of cider from his flask. 'Blummin' world's gone crazy,' he muttered to himself, and carried on extending the turret roof.

'Ma'am?' said a voice behind Tooley. She span around.

Seer Fanta and his interpreter stood behind her.

'What do you want?' she asked crossly.

The magician gabbled and the interpreter said: 'My master is distressed to see a lady so unhappy.'

'My heart bleeds for him but I'll get over it,' she retorted. She leaned her great weight back against a water butt. 'You can tell him that it he wants to cheer me up he can sling his hook.' The interpreter conferred once more with the Seer.

'My master says,' he said, turning, 'it is all the more upsetting because you are so beautiful.'

'Leave it out,' snapped the other irritably. 'I know what nature made me and I'm quite happy with it.'

'He says also,' translated the interpreter, 'that you are a wonderful cook.'

'Yeah — with nowhere to cook in.'

'And...and very wise,' the interpreter added, a small note of desperation to his voice.

Tooley's hands, which were wringing her dirty apron,

paused for just a fraction of a second. 'And pray what would your master know about being wise?' she asked cautiously.

Magician and interpreter whispered hurriedly. The latter turned back to Tooley. 'My master says he can see where the true force in this castle lies. He imagines that even the Lord himself most probably followed solely your advice.'

The cook rubbed her nose. 'Well, we did have a good natter now and then, that's for sure.'

'And you did advise him to go on his adventure, did you not?' said the interpreter, drawing closer.

'Oh, yes I did. And now look what's gone and happened.' Interpreter and Seer came to stand either side of her as Tooley brushed at another tear.

'Your master will surely be back soon enough,' the interpreter said with a strained smile. 'Until then, however, the castle will need your wisdom to see it through. It is time to take matters in hand — and to earn the respect you so richly deserve.'

Tooley's eyes glimmered with hope for an instant. Then she broke. 'But now that Grimble's in my kitchen — and there's only one of me.'

'Then why not move upstairs?' said the interpreter, barely repressing an ominous grin of satisfaction. 'You could invite some friends of your own...'

'And that's just what she did, the soft old butternut,' said Ummond, staring fixedly at Marcus Grool. 'She moved upstairs into the caretaker's quarters and all her sherry-drinking, emotionally unbalanced, bridge-playing pals came to stay.'

'And so then what happened?' asked Marcus with an apprehensive glance at the candle on the desk.

'Happened? Hah!' cried the Doctor. He leaned forward. '*Nothing* happened. That's just the point – it was a disaster. The caretaker's lot couldn't cook an egg if they accidentally dropped one in a boiling cauldron, and O' Marge and her chums quite merrily messed up all the accounts and wouldn't have known which way was west if you gave them a compass and told them to watch the sunset. Never mind the other servants.'

'What did they do?'

'Elbows Mick got so drunk and so fat he could barely get out of bed in the morning, let alone up a ladder. Very soon the castle looked like something out of a bad ghost story – pink roof, ridiculous turrets and all. And as for Nitch – zooks. The poor man was so worn out, what with providing services for dozens of visitors and looking after his sot of a cousin, that he had several nervous breakdowns.

When that happened, the whole castle froze, and if they didn't get him back on his feet pronto... Well.' The Doctor raised his eyebrows. 'It was touch and go, I tell you. And as for that Spanish imp – but we're coming to him.' Ummond sighed. He had a strange, faraway look in his eyes. 'All this went on for ten, long years.'

'Ten years?' exclaimed Marcus. 'But that's absurd, I mean – didn't they realise nothing was working properly?'

'That's just the thing,' said the Doctor, snapping back into focus. 'They all managed to convince themselves everything was perfect; except Nitch, of course, poor man. You must remember that by now that Fanta fellow had been doing the rounds and most of the other castles were in a similar way, or worse. Thus it all seemed relatively normal. Grimble got it into his head he was a genius Masterchef and O' Marge – with the help of a little sherry, you understand – thought she was Miss Organised Businesswoman of the Decade. The fact they were bankrupt and starving with the castle falling down around their ears didn't occur to them. Elbows Mick tried to say so once or twice but they just shut him up with more cider. And if by chance they ever *did* for a moment open their eyes and try their old job again' – the Doctor scratched his ear – 'their friends talked them out of it.'

Marcus sat in silence and thought. Then he looked up. 'And the Lord?'

'Ah – the Lord,' repeated Ummond. His face fell serious. 'Never heard from him again. No more letters: nada.'

'What? That – that can't be right.'

'They thought they were their own Lords,' said the Doctor. 'Aided, of course, by Seer Fanta, who wandered about the land licking the bottom of every upturned pail. So it was extremely sad,' concluded Ummond, reaching out a hand, 'yet not entirely surprising, that on the day the candle went out in the tower' – he snuffed – 'no one even noticed.'

Marcus returned home in a subdued, pensive mood – a mood that was for him quite alien. He could not figure out why, but he did not sleep at all well that night.

6

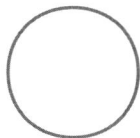

O, YOU'RE BRIGHT and early today, Mr Grool,' the receptionist chirruped when he returned a week later.

'Yes, I-' Marcus appeared rather flustered. He pushed his normally well-kempt hair from his eyes.

'My, my,' tutted the big old lady. 'You seem in a bit of a tizzy. Can I..?'

'No, that's fine,' cut in Marcus. 'I mean: thank you. Is he in?'

The receptionist looked at him with a strange, half-smile. 'The Doctor's always in, Mr Grool.' She held him for a second longer. Then she relaxed back with a creak in her chair. 'Go on, then. Quick as you like.'

Upstairs, Marcus passed a slight, elderly electrician who was fiddling with some wires in the skirting board.

The younger man nodded a hello and the electrician smiled quickly before resuming his task. Arriving hurriedly at the end of the corridor, Marcus knocked on Edmond Ummond's door and entered.

'Zeeks squeaks!' cried the Doctor. 'You're early, Grool. Is it the Day of Judgment?' Dr Ummond was not, as he was usually, behind his desk. He was standing in front of the closet that stood against the wall adjacent to the door. The other's swift entrance had evidently taken him by surprise. He hastily closed and locked the closet door.

Marcus laid his overcoat on the chest by the other wall. 'Sorry,' he said. 'I didn't mean to startle you, it's just that...' Marcus hesitated where he stood, unsure of whether to continue. Then he sat quickly down. 'I've been having some funny moments,' he managed intently at last.

The Doctor took up his habitual position without a word. He cleared away the watch mechanism and lit the candle.

'It's like,' the other went on, 'I'll be walking down the street and I'll see a sign in the window, or smell a particular smell, and suddenly my mood changes and I forget what I've been thinking about. And the strangest thing is that it doesn't matter that I've forgotten. Just for a few seconds, that sign or smell or whatever is the only important thing in the world. I get an odd sort of sensation in my stomach, like I can almost place it' — he froze, brow furrowed, fist clenched — 'and then it goes again.' Marcus relaxed. 'It's never happened to me before,' he said quietly. 'Do you know what it is?'

Dr Ummond did not respond straight away. He looked at Marcus knowingly with those clear, sea-green eyes. Then he clicked his tongue and chuckled before resuming his typically grave countenance. 'What's the name of the tavern down the high street?' he snapped.

'The — the?'

'You know: the Elizabethan mock-up with the fancy sign?'

'I don't…'

'How many names on the buzzer downstairs?' pursued the Doctor. Again, he met with a blank. 'Name of the watchmaker? No looking out the window. Well?'

'I don't know,' confessed Marcus, puzzled.

'Nah. And even if you did you wouldn't remember how to spell it.' Ummond stared at him.

'I don't understand your point,' said the young man disappointedly.

'This is your fourth visit here, isn't it Grool? Not much around to look at down our way. Not much to remember for a person who's clever enough to work in a bank.' Marcus felt suddenly crestfallen. The Doctor was right. He should at least have remembered one of the things he'd pointed out. 'What was the sign, Grool?' continued the Doctor, more gently this time. 'The one that made you feel all funny?'

'Um, it was a sign for Old Jessop's strawberry jam,' he said without hesitation. Ummond said nothing. Marcus began: 'I think it was-'

'Shh,' went the Doctor. His voice became all at once strangely different. Almost soft. Marcus was quite taken by surprise. 'It's a beginning,' the old man said. His eyes held Marcus enthralled. 'Between you and I, my boy,' he went on, 'I'd say something's a-stirring up in the tower. Leave it for the moment, lad. You'll know when the time comes.' The other blinked. A second later, Dr Ummond's normal voice suddenly returned, blasting. 'You'll not forget strawberry jam in a hurry, will you now, eh?'

'N-No,' stammered Marcus.

'D' you get that job, then?' The young man frowned for a second, then shook his head. 'Well, never mind. It'll all happen. Now where were we? Ah yes: things rotten in Ude. Candle's down and the chips are burned. And would you know, the very same morning after the candle died, a stranger arrived at the castle...'

Tooley O' Marge went down to the castle gate as usual to put letters in the box and check for any post.

Since the departure of nearly all the Lords of Ude ten years before, none of the castles left behind had been able to see one another on account of the dark, tangled forests between them. Thus, over time, a sort of messaging system had emerged between all the remaining servants so that the castles could continue to communicate. The system did not work very well.

Part of the trouble was that after such a length of time, almost all of the households had gone topsy-turvy and no one could ever be quite sure to whom they were writing. One might send a message intended for the caretaker and the cook would receive it in their stead. Or, if it did arrive in the correct hands, there was no guarantee as to who had sent it. It could have been the keeper of the beasts posing as the cook, or the mason, for instance. To complicate things further, every Lordless castle was now crammed to bursting with visitors, none of whom could ever stop scribbling messages. And then the handwriting was illegible – and so on it went.

In spite of all this, the volume of mail going back and forth continued ever to increase, and on this particular morning, Tooley could barely fit it all in the sack she carried for just this purpose. The cook was thinner now, though by no means slim, and she wore plain, business-like clothes instead of her greasy old apron. She had also grown harder in spirit, yet one would still recognise the occasional twinkle in her pale blue eyes. Tooley was just about to go back inside the castle walls when something in the ditch outside caught her attention. Glancing up and down the road she approached it tentatively. 'Well, bless me,' she breathed as she got up close.

Lying in the ditch was a man. He was dressed in the rags of a beggar and was spattered with mud and filth from head to foot. His feet were bare and in a sorry state. He had long, matted hair and a thick beard, and he appeared to be either dead or sound asleep. His lips were tinged blue with cold.

Tooley hesitated, unsure what to do. She did not really want him in the castle. They had enough mouths to feed as it was without putting up some luckless vagrant. What use could he possibly be to them anyway? And then, what if he turned out to be a thief – or even something worse? There had been dark rumours of late of servants from destitute castles running wild, pillaging and looting to survive. One had to be alert and defensive all the time these days. Was this just a trick? Tooley looked worriedly about once more in case anyone should suddenly jump out from the woods at the roadside. The only movement was the occasional drop as the morning frost melted slowly from the long grass. She could not banish the thought entirely, though. He might attack her visitors, or even herself. Tooley did not want to imagine the consequences.

Her eyes narrowed. Yes, and then Grimble would get the upper hand. After so long living in mayhem under the same, now violet roof, out of habit they generally got along all right these days, and servants and visitors wandered around the castle pretty much as they liked. They even supported one another once in a while. But there was still an unspoken rivalry between the caretaker and the cook. And if she made the wrong decision now…

'Tooley O' Marge, what are you thinking?' she scolded herself suddenly, breaking the train. 'I don't know what's become of you. Letting your mind wander about willy-nilly while a man freezes his fingers off,' and, squelching down into the oozing drainage channel, she turned the stranger's body to better see his face.

It was a handsome face, but one that looked aged beyond its years. The skin was possibly still soft in places, but it was grooved with deep lines that told of much suffering. As she looked, the man gave a feeble cough and then lay still again.

'Right,' said Tooley determinedly. 'That does it. You're coming with me, stranger,' and with no small effort she hoisted the thin body across her wide shoulders and went back inside the castle. The sack of messages was left forlorn and forgotten on the roadside.

*　　*　　*

Up in the library, Balthazar Grimble was holding a séance. The years had altered the caretaker little, for in truth he had ever appeared and behaved twice the age he really was. If there was any noticeable change to his exterior it was that the air of superiority he wove about his persona was even more exaggerated than before. In this instance, he was absurdly dressed in a sparkly suit and cape and resembled rather a circus ringmaster than any self-respecting caretaker, let alone major domo. A rag-tag mingle of visitors was bunched around the table at his behest, their hands interjoined. Every now and then, one or another would elbow their neighbour in a bid for more room, which action invariably resulted in bickering.

Grimble cleared his throat. 'Come along, everybody,' he said imperiously. 'No doubt the spirits are eagerly awaiting our invocation.' An uneven hush fell about the gathering. The caretaker closed his eyes. 'Spirits of the departed,' he intoned with exaggerated ceremony. 'We call upon you now to visit us in this sacred sanctuary for to answer these our questions, which are of the utmost severity and importance. Do you hear us?' There was silence.

Under the table, Balthazar Grimble's foot crept furtively sideways to a floorboard that had warped with the damp and had risen at one end. The foot's owner surreptitiously opened one, goldfish eye and quickly checked that everyone else at the table had theirs firmly shut. He gave the floorboard a push. On the other side of the room, the few remaining crystals hanging from a free-standing oil lamp tinkled noisily.

'Yes!' cried Balthazar Grimble ecstatically. 'You are here!' A ripple ran around the table. 'Dear departed friends, tell us: we, your humble incantators, wish to know the answer to this question. One tinkle for "no" – two tinkles for "yes". Tell us, spirits, please – your loyal friends who have called you back: are things going to be better tomorrow than they are today? Are we all…all right?' Grimble's face blindly searched thin air. There was a charged pause. The foot pushed once. A small gasp came from the congregation. Then a nervous quiet fell. The foot pushed again.

A cheer went up among them. 'Oh, thank you!' the caretaker cried triumphantly. Breaking from their trance, the visitors all congratulated him wildly. 'And may tomorrow bring all that we deserve and mo-' He stopped suddenly, uncertain. Over on the other side of the library the lamp had tinkled once more. Grimble looked worriedly across to where it stood. His foot was nowhere near the floorboard.

'Was there something more than just the usual question?' Ms Fawcett asked curiously.

Grimble turned to face them. He wiped a finger across

his creased brow where a sprinkle of perspiration had formed. 'I, er…' The lamp tinkled again, louder this time, as did the dusty chandelier on the ceiling. People began to shuffle and voices twitter in anxiety. Suddenly, Grimble's eyes opened wide. 'Oh my,' he breathed to himself. 'Can it be true?' He stared up at the ceiling. The entire library had by now begun to tremble. 'Spirits,' he called, raising his arms with awe. 'Is it true? Departed friends: tell me — but not, please, in a scary voice — am I dreaming? Are you really there?' The quaking reached a crescendo. It seemed to be caused by a steady, rhythmical thumping that was coming ever closer and closer to the startled little group. Everyone shut their eyes. A pane of glass fell from one of the windows. Then, there was a huge crash.

'No,' announced Tooley O' Marge. The cook looked down at the astonished Grimble, utterly unimpressed, before standing back to recover her breath. The others in the room regarded her in amazement. 'But this one's almost departed.'

All crowded around once more to see the peculiar offering Tooley had brought.

The stranger lay motionless on the table where he had been unceremoniously set down, the frost beginning to thaw from his wild, thick beard. Had the castle's old Great Dane been there at just that moment, he alone may have recognised something familiar about the half-dead man, whose soiled garments now dripped muddy drops on the library floor. Alas, the hound some years before had succumbed to the leftovers from one of Grimble's dinners, and Hamlet now resided in the great kennel in the sky.

The caretaker wrinkled his nose and stood back indignantly. 'What,' he asked, sniffing, 'is that?'

Tooley huffed. 'An apricot flan — what d' you think it is, Grimble, it's a blummin' man, innit?'

'I meant where did you get it?' responded the other tightly.

'In the ditch outside the gate. Poor fellow's half froze near solid. Now, where's that — ah, Nitch: get that fire roaring, will you?' The dogsbody, who as usual had arrived as if on cue, nodded hurriedly and set about the hearth.

'Well he can't stay here,' Grimble asserted, sitting down once more and folding his arms like a duke.

Tooley, who was removing the unconscious man's tattered shirt, did not turn her head. 'And why not?' she said dangerously.

'Because there's enough of us as it is, that's why. Besides, what'll he do? He looks emaciated.'

'Well, you never know,' replied the cook, starting at the trousers. 'He might be right useful when he's all fed up again. He may even be able to help you sit about holding hands all day. That'd be a load off, now wouldn't it?'

Grimble made a face. 'Right: it goes to the vote. Those in favour of throwing him back where he was found say "aye". Anyone else in the minority say "nay".' There was a general noise to the affirmative.

'Nay,' said Tooley and Patterson Nitch.

'Overruled.' The caretaker smiled smugly. 'The "ayes" have it. Once again.' He was just beginning to organise a disposal team, when a commanding voice came from the doorway.

'Nay,' it declared unequivocally. 'The stranger stays here.' All eyes turned.

An impossibly handsome, tall young man entered the room. He wore knee length boots and an embroidered jacket, and was shoe-horned into an indescribably tight pair of black trousers. His features were pronounced and sharp and his lips wide and full. His dark eyes smouldered like glowing hot chestnuts. He crunched at an apple as he strode languidly forward.

'This is none of your concern, Falego,' snapped the caretaker, retreating timidly. 'You have no part to play in the decision making process of this-' Grimble stopped. Further attempts at speech were futile, with two strong, gloved fingers thrust up his nose.

'What did you say, Grumble?' The Spaniard's perfect

100

chin pointed at the wriggling caretaker's forehead.

'N-Nothing,' squeaked the other.

'That,' said Falego, 'is a just what I thought. I make the decisions around here, understand? If I say he stays — he stays,' and removing his fingers from the unfortunate man's nostrils he wedged the apple core in Grimble's mouth.

'Where am I?'

Everyone looked around again.

On the table, the stranger had sat himself up. He squinted in the light and shivered.

'Bless my buns he *is* alive,' cooed Tooley in delight. 'Oh, and you'll catch your death. Grimble' — her head snapped sideways — 'give me that cloak.' He was about to protest but a look from the young Spaniard turned him to jelly. He handed the velvet mantle to Falego, who passed it to the cook.

The stranger looked about him. He remembered nothing. He was in a room that looked like it might once have been a library. There were few books in it. A fire burned beside him. He wore only his long underwear, was sitting on a table, and was extremely cold. All around him, faces he did not recognise peered in at him with curious, untrusting eyes. There was a musty smell of damp. And he remembered nothing.

'What is your name, stranger?' asked Falego courteously.

'I don't know,' the other replied, blinking.

Barging aside a couple of visitors, Tooley came eagerly forward. 'I found you just now — outside the castle gate,' she beamed. 'Iced over almost like a wedding cake, you was. How d' you get to be in such a state, then?'

'I don't...thank you,' said the stranger, reaching a hand up to his head. 'A castle, you said?'

'That's right.'

'And who is your Lord?'

Everyone looked blankly at one another. There was a pause. Then, in unison, about twenty voices chimed: 'I am'.

'We don't have one,' Tooley explained. 'We sort of take it in turns.' She nodded comfortingly. Falego stepped forward.

'If you work, you can stay.' He leaned closer, and then whispered: 'And just between you and me, I will be the master soon. *Comprendes?*' He winked.

'Yes.' The stranger nodded, unsure. 'Thank you. All of you.' He began to ease himself down off the table. Tooley helped him to the fireside and people began either to bustle round him or disperse, thinking there was nothing more to be seen.

Over by the wall, Grimble recovered himself and tried once again to appear dignified. He marched purposefully across to Falego, who was already occupied with flattering

Ms Fawcett. 'Excuse me,' broke in Grimble. 'Excuse me, you puffed plumcake.' The accused turned. 'And of what, exactly, is our latest burden going to avail himself while he is with us?'

The Spaniard shrugged. 'When he's strong, he can do the work of that cider-swilling sloth that calls himself a mason.' He smiled. 'And he can feed the beasts.'

'But — but that's your job,' protested the caretaker.

At that, Falego whipped about with such a vicious snarl that it made Grimble squeak in fright and trip backwards. 'Not anymore,' the Spaniard declared as the petrified caretaker fell flat on his back on the mouldering sofa. Falego advanced. 'I am sick of being treated like a pig-slave,' he growled. 'You people — always making me clean a this or fetch a that because you are too lazy to do your own dirty work. Well today, *amigos*, it stops. I was made for more than this. I can dance, I can sing; I romance, I swing. I' — he thumped his chest — 'am a lion.

'When God made the lion, did he give him lion's legs so he could do the work of a donkey? No. When God made the lion, did he give him a lion's tongue so he could lick the kitchen floor? No way. And when God made the lion, did he give him lion's claws, and lion's teeth, so he could burn the meringues, and nibble on after dinner mints? Absolutely not! He gave them to hunt' — he stamped — 'and to kill!' Falego paced regally to the doorway. The entire library was watching. 'I will find me some big game,' he said casually. 'I will feed the beasts no more.' He grinned a devilish smile. 'I,' he swore, '*am* the beast!' And with a flourish, he was gone.

7

I T'S YOUR FAULT he's turned out like that,' muttered Grimble later on that day. He had found Tooley staring down at the carriageway from the dining room window. They looked together now. 'You've always encouraged him.'

Below them, Falego and the stranger were walking up the drive towards the castle gate. They watched as the Spaniard pointed out the pen by the wall where the animals were kept, explaining with great gestures what was to be done. Then, with a cheek-splitting grin, he clapped the stranger on the shoulder and vanished through a gap in the rusting iron portal. The other man appeared to pause. He looked back at the castle, and up to the dark, empty tower. Then he set about his work.

Tooley's eyes narrowed. 'There's something about that

one,' she said to herself.

'For once we are in agreement,' stated Grimble beside her with a sniff. 'Any man who claims to have no name, no abode *and* refuses to shave can be only one thing: a fraudster.'

'Yeah, well aren't we lucky we got nothing left to be frauded out of, then?' the other said, turning promptly.

'If you and your rabble kept the accounts properly we'd be quite solvent,' accused Grimble, following her stiffly. 'I shan't even begin on the subject of gambling.'

'And if you hadn't given most of the silver and furniture away to Seer Fanta we could have ourselves a party,' returned the cook, heading down the stairs. 'Blazes, that reminds me: I must do those promissory notes for the debt collector before tomorrow.'

'What?' cried the caretaker, emerging eventually behind the cook from the gloomy stairwell. 'Mr Pinch is coming here again? That's preposterous.'

'Pay for all your fancy apparatus,' murmured Tooley. She scanned the kitchen, which these days resembled an exploded chemist's lab more than a place where food might be prepared. She pondered, then went into the larder.

Grimble sniffed at a half-empty flask in its stand. He wrinkled his nose. 'Besides,' he called through, 'Seer Fanta is a genius. We'd be nothing without him. Nothing.' He looked about forlornly. His brow darkened. 'And now that

Spanish reprobate has torn loose I fear for everything.'

Tooley returned with an old, cracked mixing bowl. She pumped the handle of the water pump. Nothing happened. 'Nitch!' she shouted.

'What are you up to, anyway? This is my kitchen.'

'Just reminiscing a bit, you know,' she said, smiling as at first brown and then clear, fresh water gurgled from the pipe.

'I fear for our reputation,' the caretaker continued, scrunching his knuckles. 'I fear for our lives.' His voice cracked.

'Quit whining,' reprimanded the other. 'It never does any good. And anyway, I know where he's gone off to. Gone to that castle a way along the road there.'

Grimble checked a shudder. He blinked. 'You don't mean – the one where the Lady died?'

'That's right.'

'I was never told of this.' The caretaker bristled.

'I told Mr Fusset,' replied Tooley. 'If your visitors want to keep secrets from you that's not my problem. Our Falego's got himself a fancy friend up there. Girl who feeds the swine. And you could never guess who put him up to it, could you?' Grimble swallowed. 'That's right: Seer Fanta.'

The problems with Falego had begun a couple of years before. Tooley remembered the incident vividly. She had been boxing up some of the Lord's old family candlesticks one day to pay off Mr Pinch in lieu of money they owed, and was bending down to put the lid on another crate when she felt the trace of fingers run across her broad behind. She flew about to see the Spanish boy, now full grown and handsome, flash a wicked, white smile. 'You grubby little rascal!' she shouted, reddening. 'Just what do you think you're doing?'

Falego cocked his head. 'For a woman with so much beauty,' he said smoothly, 'surely you could spare me just a little?' Tooley had beaten him back with the crate lid, but the seed was soon. Secretly, she had also been quite excited.

After that, Falego became something of a nuisance. He had always been useful for filling in on chores that were not his own (in that complaint he was quite justified) but an energy now began to grow in him that would not be quenched. He spent it on dancing and on distracting all the visitors, and though Tooley and the others were not overly perturbed by the Spaniard's frolics, which were always fun and even pleasurable, Balthazar Grimble's incisiveness could not be denied when he maintained it was wasting limited resources and that something must be done. A meeting upstairs was convened. Servants and visitors conducted a mass debate on the issue, but the results were inconsequential and only delayed the inevitable time bomb.

Then, Seer Fanta suggested the castle up the road.

The Lady who had lived in that castle a little way along the valley had formerly been betrothed to one of the departing Lords. When he failed to return, her constitution weakened and diminished day by day until, finally, she faded altogether and died. Her servants were left to the running of the household. In this instance, the cook was a kind but particularly frail and weak man and, in no time, as with so many other castles in Ude, the place was upside down. A small but savagely fierce woman who was the caretaker quickly took charge and showed little mercy or patience. In fact, the only other servant she allowed to do as she pleased was the girl who kept the swine.

The young swineherd was no exceptional beauty but she certainly had a ready sort of charm about her. Having passed through most castles of the land, Seer Fanta was well versed on the natures of their inhabitants. He remembered this rough jewel and thus, when on one of his regular visits he perceived the young Spanish boy twitching in agitation, he wasted no time in dropping morsels of information and suggestive images into the other's eager ears. Falego began slipping out regularly, and by the time the rest of either castle was aware of what was really happening, he and the girl were entrenched in the affair. So it had continued for the past four months.

Today, the young dandy was in an even brighter mood than usual as he danced along the lane. Through the force of his character, he had won the castle's consent, if not their entire approval. Yes, thought Falego, grinning in anticipation: today would be a special day indeed. He sang a merry tune for himself and plucked a wild rose from the wayside. It made him laugh. Yet of laughs, he would not have the last.

* * *

Tooley, Grimble and the rest of the household awoke in the middle of the night to the sound of wild screaming. It was coming from the castle gate. Muttering and blinking in their bedclothes, everyone went outside onto the gravel to see what was the matter. Grimble held up a lantern and squinted into the darkness. There was nothing. Then, from out of the black, a frantic figure emerged.

'Run!' bawled Falego, bursting his lungs. 'They're coming! Run away, run!' The Spaniard skidded wildly to a stop as he reached the others, scattering stones.

'What on Earth's the matter, boy?' said Tooley O' Marge, half laughing.

'Come on man: spit it out,' demanded Grimble.

'They're coming,' Falego panted.

'Who is coming?'

'All of them, I think,' he wheezed.

Tooley chortled nervously. 'All of who?'

'The dead Lady's household.' He looked at them both uncomfortably. 'And their friends,' he added. Then he glanced at the rest of the group. 'And their friends' friends.' He straightened and clasped his heaving sides. 'And maybe their friends as well,' he finished eventually.

A general murmur ran through the people assembled there in the light of the lantern. 'Well that's just ridiculous,' said Tooley, waving her hand. 'We can't possibly feed all them people.'

'I don't believe,' said Grimble, eyeing Falego, 'they are passing by on the off-chance of a late supper.' He and the Spaniard stared at one another. Finally, Falego conceded.

'She didn't like my proposal,' confessed the young man.

'Proposal? Who didn't like?'

'The battle-axe caretaker. I proposed that Mabel — that's the pig-girl, she's sweet, you'd like her — anyway, I proposed she come and live with us, you know; since you all said it was okay. She ask the caretaker what she think; the caretaker say fine in her opinion as long as the rest of the castle come too. So I give her my opinion.'

'Which was?'

'Get stuffed.'

'Falego!'

'I tell her her castle smell like the underpants of a dead Venetian sailor. She hit me. I tell her she don't hit so well. She hit me again. She say she going to get all her friends from other castles to come over to our castle and tell us what's what. I say fine, she can hit me as hard as she likes because I going to get our catapult. She hit me very hard. See?' He pointed to a trickle of blood at his mouth.

Grimble all at once looked most alarmed. 'But – but we don't possess a catapult.'

'I know.' Falego nodded. He looked up. 'But her friends do.'

The next instant, the small, midnight gathering became aware of a shrill, arching whistle somewhere high above. Straining their ears to follow it, their heads turned slowly as one, from the direction of the castle gate towards the main building behind them. There was a split pause. A couple of people raised their eyebrows. Then, there was an explosion.

'Run!' yelled Grimble as something dark and heavy smashed into the castle roof. Shards of lurid violet tiling began to fall about the carriageway. 'Run for your lives! Run!' Visitors scattered in all directions. Another missile bowled into the swollen west turret, taking the top clean off. As everyone dashed inside for cover, Grimble managed to grab the Spaniard by a torn sleeve. 'This is your fault, man, d' you hear? Your fault!' He stared up into Falego's face and seethed.

The other looked back. He arched an eyebrow. 'Okay,' he said. 'Is my fault.' As the third bomb hit, he even managed a smile. 'Now, it's your problem.'

Tooley, by this time, had already rushed down to the basement, where she found the ever alert Nitch frantically trying to rouse a comatose Elbows Mick. She seized the slumbering mason by his drool-stained overalls and shook him violently. 'Wake up, man!' she bellowed. 'We're being attacked!' Mick belched and tried to roll over in his sleep. An empty cider jar tumbled off the bed and smashed. She shook him roughly again and even clouted him across the face; but the mason could not have been more content if he were wrapped in apple-scented cotton wool. 'Right,' puffed Tooley at last, heaving herself to her feet. 'Nitch – you sort the house. I'll deal with this.'

Down by the gate, the attackers were in a savage frenzy. As another stone ploughed into the castle, they whooped and cheered like intoxicated revellers on a fairground ride. Another block was loaded. They were about to let it fly when a calm voice from inside the gateway made them pause and turn.

'Why are you doing this?' the stranger asked them.

There was some hesitancy before a small, fierce woman stepped forward and spat. 'For disrespecting our castle.' There was a strong murmur of assent.

'Who disrespected your castle?'

'The beast-boy,' rumbled a big man among them.

The stranger thought for a moment. His brow furrowed. 'And your Lady sent you to do this?' he enquired.

'We ain't got a Lady,' returned the woman. She wiped her nose with a forearm, slightly calmer.

'Then you're all looking for the same thing,' said the stranger. 'Why don't you help each other?'

'There's no help for the likes of him,' said the woman bitterly. 'He wants locking away.' She glanced at the bearded man with curiosity. 'Anyway: who are you to be standing here in the middle of the night, doling out cheap advice like it's Christmas?' There was a pause. Slowly, the stranger said:

'I don't know.'

'That figures. I wouldn't hang around here too long if I were you. They're a rum lot, that bunch.' The small woman looked around. She appeared all at once strangely mollified. 'All right. Come on you lot. That'll do for tonight.' With a few odd looks aside at the stranger, the attackers wheeled away the catapult and began to drift back into the night. An earthy, attractive looking girl was left last of all.

'Where's your Lady?' the stranger asked gently.

The girl regarded him. Her expression was one of part suspicion, but also part curious fascination. 'Our Lady's dead,' she replied at last. The two stood together in silence a few moments, looking at one another. The girl was not the only one fascinated. Then, after a little while longer, she smiled coyly and with a turn of her long skirts disappeared off up the road.

The stranger continued to stand there for a minute or two, simply staring. Eventually he heard a noise behind him. He turned to find Tooley O' Marge. In each of the woman's big hands, a homemade grenade from Grimble's chemistry equipment burned smokily. Tooley panted to a halt.

'Well, bless me,' she exclaimed softly. She glanced at the stranger suspiciously. 'They've run off.'

'What happened to your Lord, Tooley?' the stranger asked.

The cook thought for a moment. Then, as if suddenly remembering, she cast a look back towards the castle, up at the tower. No light came from it. Tooley's mouth trembled, at once uncontrollable, as though a forgotten tank full of emotion had finally burst and now began to flood through her. When she turned to the stranger again, she had tears running down her face. 'His Lordship died,' she said brokenly. The grenades puffed out with a hiss. Softly, it began to rain.

'The stranger's first night in the beast house wasn't exactly luxury,' said Dr Ummond, 'but at least he didn't spend it alone. It was the only dry roof on the property, and all spent a very cosy, pungent evening together. Well.' He drummed on the arms of his chair.

'They should have got hold of that Falego character and locked him in the basement,' said Marcus with a stretch.

'Worst thing they could do,' countered the Doctor. 'Repression in that manner becomes denial, the most dangerous thing of the lot. He'd have sent everyone mad with his shouting, and if he didn't get loose — which he probably would have — he'd have poisoned them all as he festered. Take it from me, Grool: if you can't correct something, best let it go. Never repress. Never.'

Marcus studied his hands. 'It was just an opinion,' he mumbled, slightly wounded.

The Doctor's eyes became slits. 'What was that word?' he hissed.

'I said it was only an opinion.'

Ummond pointed a bony finger. 'Never use that word in front of me again, Grool. D' you understand?' He snuffed the candle.

Marcus, feeling somewhat riled by now at all the sudden hostility, decided he would not let this one drop. 'What's wrong with having an opinion?' he said defensively. 'Everyone has opinions. It's what makes us human.'

'No!' To the other's real surprise, Ummond thumped the desk with the flat of his hand so quickly, and with such force, that the shock made the window rattle. He regarded the Doctor worriedly. 'It's exactly what stops you from being human and makes you into a damn robot!' the old man shouted. 'It's the very reason you're here, you great imbecile. It's why you can't see beyond your nose. So when I say I don't want to hear your opinion, that's exactly what I mean. You came here to listen. If I want an opinion I'll read the newspaper.' He opened a drawer and slammed it shut again angrily. By now, however, Marcus was burning.

'Listen,' he said, shaking, 'I don't care if you are much older than me, or much cleverer, or anything; but I'm paying you a lot of money for this and I'm trying my hardest, so if I'm told I can't have an opinion then I want to know why.'

'All right, then,' snapped Ummond, afire. Both men were now on their feet. 'You wanna get stung, laddie, I'll sting ya. Just what is an opinion?'

'An opinion's a judgment,' said Marcus, thinking fast.

'Hah!'

'A – a judgment based on fact.'

'Brilliant!' shrieked Ummond at the ceiling. 'What's a fact when it's at home?'

'Something that's objective,' riposted the patient, 'that just is. Something everyone agrees on.'

'Oh – you mean one, big mass opinion?' gleamed the Doctor. 'Let's take it back a way: the world is flat, the Sun moves round the Earth, matter is solid; women are stupid. That sort of fact?' He jabbed a digit. 'You give me one fact and I swear to you I'll dance naked on the windowsill.'

'A fact is something you can confirm,' grated Marcus. 'Something you just know.'

'Wonderful!' the Doctor cried. 'Give me one.'

'What?'

'One fact.'

Marcus frowned. 'I can give you hundreds,' he said.

'One will do, don't kill yourself in my office,' said Ummond, waving a hand.

Marcus bristled. 'All right,' he said firmly: 'I am a man.'

'I am a man,' the Doctor repeated, sitting himself down again. He ground his cracked teeth together for a moment or two. Then he said: '"I" – let's start with "I". Who is that?'

'Me – Marcus Grool.'

'What – the Marcus Grool who's responsible and works hard in a bank or the one who cuts all his suits into little pieces? The one who gets angry when you push all his buttons or the one who squares up to a challenge and goes back to the quack even though he's a raving lunatic? The one who forgets everything he sees or the one with a thing for strawberry jam?' Ummond paused, fixedly. He continued: 'Is that the Marcus Grool I see, your boss sees, your parents see, your friends see or is it the one your girlfriend sees and, if she's lucky, occasionally even gets a bit of loving from?'

'Now just you-'

'"Am",' pronounced the Doctor. 'What part of the verb is that? I'll save you the trouble: first person singular, present indicative active of the verb "to be" — *active*, Grool; not the motion of being passively washed along on the vomitous tide of accident, being made to feel all sorts of things you don't want to feel until you get thrown up, beached and lambasted by some geriatric despot simply because you never learned how to think. Being is doing, Grool, and what's more is the first duty of every one of us.

'We'll skip the indefinite article as it'll only confuse you and go straight on with the star prize: "man". What's a man?'

'This,' Marcus said feebly. 'Flesh and blood.'

'Flesh and blood, eh? Maybe to you. To a Buddhist your body's an illusion. A man's what's trapped inside.'

'I'm not a Buddhist.' Marcus trembled, but not from anger.

'No, you're not,' the Doctor said sharply. 'But a fact is

something everybody agrees on, isn't it? To a Christian, flesh and blood is a gift of the Divine, which is why they murdered all the Cathars, among others, who believed it was a piece of Hell. Difference of opinion, note. A Darwinist will call you a lucid ape whereas an Egypt conspirator might say you're the result of a cosmic genetic experiment. An alien would no doubt call you a dysfunctional alien where an ant would see you as a colossal agent of destruction; a biologist would quite possibly tell you you're a tight community of highly organised cells and to a quantum physicist you might be nothing more than a bunch of very tiny bits of string. And speaking of string,' said the Doctor, leaning closer, 'answer me this, factual question: just how long, Grool, is a piece of string?' He sat back again and stared. Then he looked out of the window. 'We're overtime but don't panic – I won't make you pay for it.'

'I'm me,' Marcus said brokenly. 'I'm Marcus Grool.'

'We're back where we started.' Dr Ummond sucked his tongue in a casual manner. He tapped his desk. 'Go on, man. Go home, whatever you are. Take your opinions with you.'

Without saying a word, Marcus rose from his chair and left.

8

'ARE YOU GOING to see Dr Ummond today?' asked Elizabeth.

Marcus sat on a stool in his bathrobe, staring and drinking coffee. The pretty, young teacher watched him from the corner of one eye as she prepared herself for school. He looked tired and had several days' growth of stubble. When he turned to face his girlfriend, it was as though he was emerging from a trance. 'I...I don't know,' Marcus mumbled.

'Still upset about last time?' Elizabeth checked for something in her handbag.

'A bit, I suppose. Yes.'

Remembering, the teacher walked behind him and fetched her phone from the charger. She put the mobile in her bag. 'Not fair,' she uttered, double-checking. 'Is it?'

Marcus looked at her. Then he sighed. 'It's not quite like that,' he said, raising his cup. 'It's different somehow.'

'Well. I'm going to be late,' Elizabeth said. She moved around the counter and kissed him. 'Oo – bristles. I'll get you some more razors.'

'I'll do that,' said Marcus as she walked to the door. Before she reached it, he asked, 'Beth?' She paused. 'How's that kid doing? You know: the one whose father's sick?'

'Oh. Justin.' Elizabeth relaxed and cocked her head slightly. 'He's... he's okay.' Marcus nodded and returned to his coffee.

Surprised, but not unpleasantly so, Elizabeth went off to work.

When Marcus arrived at No. 73 the door was already open. A burly old builder was giving it a once over with a lick of new paint. 'Afternoon,' said the builder. Marcus returned the greeting. He was just about to go in when something made him pause, and he turned to look across the street. Then he had an idea.

'Afternoon, Doctor.'

'Ah, Grool.' Dr Ummond cleared away the broken pocket watch as usual. 'Wasn't so sure you'd be back this time,' he said quietly after a pause. 'Go on, have a seat, man.'

The other hesitated. Then he came forward, producing a small package from his coat pocket. 'Actually, I got you something.'

'Oh, really?' Ummond's white eyebrows arched up towards the top of his head. Marcus handed him the parcel and went to put his coat on the chest by the door. The Doctor opened the little packet with dexterous precision and let the contents drop out onto his hand. It was a watch.

'I bought it from Mr Meztchek across the road,' explained Marcus, looking on. The Doctor caught his eye. He gave a quick chortle.

'Very good,' he said. 'Zooks! It beeped at me.'

'Yes – it's, er, computerised,' said Marcus, coming around the other side of the desk to show the old man. 'See? It has a stopwatch, calendar – that sort of thing.' The two men regarded the crystal screen as Ummond made the watch beep and numbers blink. 'In case you ever can't find your matches,' added the younger with a small smile. He returned to his place. Dr Ummond smacked his lips, still fiddling.

'My my. What will they think of next?' He looked the timepiece over once more and then strapped it to his skinny wrist. 'Well. Thank you very much. Very kind of you.' Marcus smiled awkwardly. Ummond continued to stare. Then he got to his feet and went to the window. 'I want to apologise to you, Grool,' he said, looking out.

The other shifted. 'Doctor, really it's-'

'Just — just hear me out, please, will ya?' There was a small silence. Turning around, Ummond said: 'I've been in my line of work a long time, you see? Contrary to the popular view, I get far more failures than I do success stories. The unfortunate truth is there's not much can be done with most people nowadays. Poor creatures' heads are so full of rubbish they think up is red and a beefburger tastes like champagne. If you try to show them otherwise, they think you're trying to trick them, or something.' He pressed his thin lips together tightly. Then he returned to his chair.

'So,' he continued, 'it gets me most frustrated when a potential success story goes and gets themselves hooked up on something half way through. But that's no excuse. And I want to say I'm sorry. I may be fruity but I can't blame it on senility. Went through that one years ago.'

'It's all right,' said Marcus. 'It's just that — well. You do take a bit of getting used to.'

'Hah!' The Doctor clicked. 'You may be right. Come and look at this.' Marcus leaned across inquisitively as Ummond searched for and found his old matchbox. 'Now watch.' He struck a flame and put it gently to the wick of the candle on the desk. It caught with a crackle and spit. 'When you light a candle,' demonstrated Ummond, 'you get

a big flame, then a small flame; then a big flame again. See?'
The other nodded. 'Why do you think that is?'

Marcus thought. 'Because...the flame first has to melt the wax?'

'Very good, Grool,' the Doctor cried. 'See? You're not a moron after all.' He sat back once more and folded his hands. 'I have to know what kind of wax I've got to work with,' he said, a canny glint in his sea-green eyes. 'I've only got so many matches. And so much time,' he added as an afterthought.

The young man looked up at him. 'And – and that's why you're always so rude to me?' he asked.

'Life rule three hundred and sixty-something: the man who shouts at you is not necessarily your enemy. And' – Ummond squinted one eye – 'the man who smiles isn't always your friend.'

'I haven't always been brilliant with people,' confessed Marcus gloomily. 'Elizabeth always seems to get it right, but I...' He held up his hands.

The Doctor was nodding his head. 'Yes, well women often know,' he agreed. 'Smartest creatures alive, bless 'em. Teacher well?'

'A bit stressed.'

'That's why she needs you fit and dandy,' said Ummond. 'Goodness, you don't know how much time you can waste

125

being unfit for them, Grool. Then one day – "Zip!" – they're gone.' There was a pause as the Doctor stared into air, unfocused. Then he chuckled dryly.

'What?' said Marcus with a frown.

'I was just thinking,' replied Ummond, 'this is usually the point in the cliché where you ask if I've ever had a girl, following which I break out the old romantic loser's sob story.'

'Oh,' said Marcus, raising his eyebrows. He pondered for a second; concentrated. As casually as he was able, he said: 'So – did you once have a girl?'

'None of your nosy business,' snapped Ummond. 'Let's get on.'

Although slightly disappointed not to hear something of the Doctor's past life for a change, Marcus could not refrain from smiling. 'You know "To be" isn't an active verb,' he said, watching for a reaction.

'I suppose you got *that* from one of those fancy dictionary things.' Marcus nodded. 'Well – never believe everything you read,' Ummond said, scratching. 'Quickest way to madness, believe you me. Now, are you ready? Good. Autumn became winter, and it wasn't long before everyone living in the castle became very miserable indeed...'

The once proud and strong fortress was an extremely sorry spectacle. The attack had all but demolished the roof and, seeing as Elbows Mick was too bloated to even make it out of the basement, the rest of the servants and visitors had to come up with a solution for themselves. None was particularly well versed in the art of masonry and eventually they just hauled an old tarpaulin over the remaining beams and weighed it down with rubble against the wind. Their labours were not entirely successful. Everyone was soon damp and chill and tetchy and the general mood was thoroughly depressing.

Grimble began to disagree with anyone about anything and at length started holding long and verbose discourses with himself. Tooley turned to the sherry and sunk deeper into her gambling at cards, and poor Patterson Nitch was buried under such an immense weight of work that he had to be resuscitated twice. As for Falego: the cause of their latest misfortune was forbidden by a majority vote to leave the castle grounds. He slinked about the peeling rooms, trying to persuade people with his usual charms to let him out just one last time.

Had he succeeded, the Spaniard would not have gotten far. Almost all the other nearby castles had heard of his exploits and as a result wanted nothing to do with either him or his household in general. The messages at the gate reduced to a trickle and eventually ceased entirely. They were cut off from the rest of Ude, and consequently no one had the desire to do any work at all, given the bleakness of future prospects. The once warm, welcoming, feasting merry home sank ever more sullenly into decline and closed its doors to all.

Only the stranger appeared to remain relatively unfazed. He by and large kept to himself down in the beasts' pen where he worked and slept, and he observed the goings on dispassionately and with little comment. This non-judgmental trait of his character after a while attracted Tooley's attention and, when she was not busy either drinking or gambling – or both – she would often sneak down for a good old moan and a chat with the mystery visitor. He was an extremely patient listener. He spoke little in return, however, for of his own story he still remembered nothing. His conversation was usually limited to observations and questions about how the castle had been before the Lord's disappearance.

'Why don't you go back to running it as it was?' he asked once.

Tooley laughed. 'Oh, we could never be doing that,' she chuckled. 'We's far too used to things the way they are now.'

'It sounds as if it was a much happier place then.'

'It was.' The cook sighed with a heave of her great bosom. 'Oh, it was.' She looked at the stranger seriously. 'But, truth is, I don't think any of us has got the will enough for it anymore.'

Weeks passed. Nothing improved. The castle turrets sagged and collapsed but no one noticed. Falego got out and on his return brought with him an infestation of lice. And when Seer Fanta and his insalubrious band came and removed the last, precious books from the library, Grimble was so oblivious that the magician and his followers could not refrain from laughing. 'I am a king,' cheeped the caretaker vacantly from where he sat, legs tucked beneath him, like a canary in the empty alcove. He stared into space. 'Tomorrow, I shall be a god.' The Seer smiled. Nodding knowingly to his acolytes, he left.

One day, Tooley asked the stranger to come inside the castle. 'I've a sneaking suspicion,' she said, waddling up the stairs ahead of him, 'that you can do more than just take care of them beasts.'

The stranger looked about him as he followed, picking his way through visitors who sat huddled in ones and twos in the corridor, chattering with cold. They passed the library, where Grimble was arguing noisily with himself, and then the dining room. The great hall was damp and bare of furniture. A bracing wind blew through the broken lead windows. Everything was grey. 'Here we are,' said Tooley cheerily. She pulled on a craftily concealed bottle of sherry.

They had arrived in the study. It was empty, save for junk and broken packing boxes, and a single, old bureau that was crammed with yellowing sheaves of paper. To this latter the cook now trundled over. 'Now what I'd got to thinking,' she said, retrieving wadges of letters and bill slips, 'was that a smart young man like yourself could do us a favour and just have a double check of these accounts. I'm a bit busy at the moment, you see?' she said, adding a hiccup.

'I can neither read nor write, I'm afraid,' said the stranger, though he said it absently for something he had not noticed at first now caught his attention. 'At least, I don't remember being able to,' he continued, advancing towards the object that intrigued him.

Tooley's face fell. 'Oh,' she said, her hands full of paper. 'Pop goes that soufflé.'

The stranger reached the painting and stopped. Carefully, he raised a rough, dirty hand and brushed the cobwebs from the canvass. A handsome face looked out at him. It was a young man with fair, wavy hair and an expression that conveyed energy and assuredness, combined with deep sensibility. The sea was in the background, and the eyes held a look that hinted at memories of many a long-watched Moon. 'Is this your master, Tooley?' the stranger murmured.

'What? Oh, yes. That were 'im,' she said sadly. 'Handsome devil, wasn't he?'

The stranger continued to stare. 'Did he do anything important?'

'He just was important,' replied the cook, coming forward to stand beside the other. 'He knew how things should be done, if you catch my meaning – and by whom. He knew what was what. Ah, he were a live one.' She gazed up fondly at the flaking image. 'Oo, and he made candles in the tower, of course.'

The stranger blinked. He frowned. 'The tower?' he said, turning.

Stranger and cook stood together before the foreboding, expectant oak wood door. The stranger tried the heavy handle. It turned, but the door did not budge. 'No one's been up there in over ten years,' Tooley whispered, glancing uneasily about. 'It were only his Lordship knew where the key was. He was the only one who ever went up there, you see?'

'I wonder where he put it,' mused the other, turning to survey their surroundings. His eyes wandered over the cold, featureless corridor. There was a strange, almost unnatural stillness here that was not to be found in other parts of the castle. Almost as if the very stones were watching, waiting, for something. But for what? The sharp light that slanted in like white razors through the arrow slits proffered no suggestions.

The stranger faced the door again. He ran his fingers over the rough wooden surface. Combined with the prescient atmosphere in the corridor, it produced a most peculiar sensation within him – like a déjà-vu. His brow creased.

'You all right?' asked Tooley, noticing his expression.

Where would *I* have put it, the stranger thought? Where would... From nowhere, all at once an image leaped into his mind. Its unexpectedness made him reel. He winced and dropped to his knees. He saw before him an iron key... then candles...a telescope...a girl...

'Oh my word!' cried Tooley worriedly. 'Sir, are you all right?'

The stranger shook for a second. The images blazed, then faded. His eyes snapped up, burning. 'What did you just call me?' he breathed.

'I don't-' Tooley stopped short. Her own eyes widened. For an instant, stranger and cook stared at one another, almost crazed. There was something there, a thread between them: so near – so real... Then a voice behind them broke the spell.

'She call you what she should call me,' it said. 'Miss Marge – we really need to talk.' From the shadow of the passageway, the forlorn figure that was Falego stepped into the light. His hair was dishevelled, his clothes stained, and his hands held securely together by a pair of thumb-cuffs.

Tooley straightened and shook herself from her trance. 'And just what is there to talk about?' she asked, returning to her usual self and marching briskly past the beleaguered Spaniard. She headed back towards the study. Behind them, the stranger rose shakily to his feet.

'This is simply not fair,' Falego wailed, shaking his coupled hands at her as he followed. 'When God made the lion, did he give him a roar to make tremble in a cage? I-'

'Shush your noise,' cut in Tooley. 'Because of you I've been itching for a fortnight. And fair in life's what you pay to the coachman. Lions included. Now. 'Less you've got anything useful to say I suggest you go back to your pit.'

'I want to go out.'

'Not useful. Down.'

'I need to play,' he pleaded, almost sobbing. 'Look at us: we have no life; we have no laughter; we have nothing to...to tickle,' he snapped, pulling at his bonds. 'Just let me visit one more castle, just one. I promise it will be the last, I swear.'

'Thanks to you, Casanova,' said the cook tersely as she plumped herself in front of the study bureau, 'none of the other castles will have anything to do with us. There's only one in the valley you haven't visited, and you're not going there.'

'Why not?' panted Falego angrily.

'Because,' replied Tooley, vainly trying to sort through the chaos before her, 'a Princess lives there, and while you may dress like a peacock you're still nothing more than a jay bird.'

Falego appeared, more than anything, supremely puzzled by this remark.

'Invite her here.'

The servants turned.

The stranger stood in the doorway. He looked suddenly most serious and insistent. 'But – but that's impossible,' the cook began to protest.

'Nothing is impossible,' replied the stranger, coming towards them, 'and it's the only thing in the world that is. Look around us, Tooley. There are crates we can turn into furniture, and all Grimble's old instruments we can use for cutlery and glass. You don't need the fancy costumes for anything that matters: we can turn them into drapes, and curtains and tablecloths for the dining room. There are beasts in the pen we can slaughter, and I'll wager that between yourself and Elbows Mick there's enough liquor stashed away around here to float an armada.' Tooley flushed beetroot. 'We can do it,' vowed the stranger, regarding them intently, 'if we all work together.'

'But why?' flustered the cook. 'Why should we ask the Princess over here?'

The stranger's eyes twinkled. 'Because, Tooley O' Marge,' he said, 'everyone needs a light to follow.'

Falego smiled from ear to ear. 'It is a brilliant idea,' he declared with a bow to the stranger. Under his breath, he added: 'And the lion will roar again.'

9

AFTER SO LONG spent in frozen torpor, now it was as though a warm breath floated through the castle and gently thawed the frost from every surface and creature there. Upon hearing the idea, Grimble emerged like a child from his twittering solipsism and immediately began to organise the visitors into task forces. Elbows Mick was dragged unceremoniously from his den of sloth and roundly told there would be no more cider until he picked himself up and mended the roof. The incentive proved remarkably effective.

Tooley O' Marge took up her former role in the kitchen. She found her old apron, still perfectly crumpled and dirty, hidden away in the larder and at first was in quite a flap as to where everything was and what to do. Patterson Nitch stoked up a furnace of a fire, however, and soon she was cracking eggs and mixing flour as though she had never stopped. She bustled ceaselessly about the kitchen, every once in a while exclaiming: 'Oh, where did I put that pan?' or 'Now look, Tooley O' Marge, the pot's gone and boiled over.' Meanwhile, Grimble and Falego, the latter as ever under duress, performed alchemy of a kind by turning instruments into eating utensils. The stranger brought in the food to be cooked and occasionally, though none including himself noticed this was happening, when asked a question would give them all advice.

Eventually, the place was set. The dining room, though not decorated in a fashion as would please any lifestyle magazine, looked nevertheless warm and inviting. A fire crackled in the hearth, curtains covered the missing panes in the windows and, with the help of oil spared from the cooking, the soft, yellow glow of lamplight filled the room.

Considering his state of health, Elbows Mick had done an admirable job on the castle's exterior. He replaced all the tiles that had not been smashed completely in the attack and filled in the rest with ones salvaged from the fallen turrets. Architecturally, the result was a touch peculiar, leaving the castle looking not dissimilar to a violet-speckled frog. The impromptu dressing of the windows with some old Christmas tinsel Mick had found caused yet further debate.

Nonetheless, the main parts of the building were warm and dry, although to the exhausted mason's disgruntlement he was informed there would be no more cider until the evening of the dinner itself.

The only task remaining was to invite the Princess. Falego had to be physically restrained from bolting out of the door and the thumb-cuffs were quickly replaced. Grimble asserted that he or one of his visitors should do the asking on account of their "superior knowledge with regards to the proper usage of language". The idea was generally well-received. However, at the last minute the stranger, who had been watching from the corner in the kitchen, suggested instead that perhaps it should be Tooley who went over to make the invitation in person.

'And pray why,' asked the caretaker haughtily, 'should an ignorant cook do the job of a genius?'

The stranger thought. 'Well, Mr Grimble,' he replied at length, 'if I were a Princess, I think I would be quite tired of meeting geniuses and hearing the proper usage of language. Don't you?' He arched an eyebrow playfully. Then his face softened. 'Let Tooley do it. She knows what's what.' Tooley blushed with pride.

An hour or so later, however, the cook returned in quite a fluster. 'Oh dear,' she puffed, sighing with a "crack" onto a chair in the kitchen. All crowded around.

'What is it? Is she coming?' they enquired anxiously.

Tooley fanned her face with a fat hand. 'Oh, she's coming all right.'

'Then why do you sweat like a meatball?' asked Falego with a frown.

'When she'd heard where I'd come from,' explained Tooley, glancing sharply at the Spaniard, 'the Princess herself came out to meet me. Oh, she's a special one, she is. Such a beauty.' Falego's teeth shone. 'Anyway, she was so excited, I thought she were gonna explode. Well, I says to meself, that's a fine job done Tooley O' Marge. We'll have a right rip-roarer tonight. Then she asked me if his Lordship had returned.' She paused; swallowed.

'Well?' squeaked Ms Fawcett.

'What did you tell her? Spit it out, woman.'

'I said *yes*,' said Tooley. She looked about worriedly. 'I thought if I told her no, she wouldn't want to come no more.'

'See?' Grimble folded his arms sanctimoniously. 'That's what happens when you send a cook to do the Major Domo's job.'

'What will we do?' asked one of the visitors. An unsettled murmur now ran through those assembled in the kitchen. Grimble scratched nervously at his wrinkled brow.

'Well there's nothing else for it,' he announced. 'I shall just have to assume the role of his Lordship.' He brushed at his nose. 'No doubt the undertaking will pose little difficulty.'

'Wrong!' All turned as Falego rose irascibly from his seat. He towered over the caretaker. 'Everybody knows that a Lord must have passion, have courage and fire. You, Grumble,' he sneered, 'have all the fire of a frozen fishstick. *I* shall be the Lord.' The Spaniard scanned the faces about him, daring anyone to challenge.

Tooley sighed. 'I'm afraid he's right, Balthazar,' she said, rising also. 'You are a bit — well — *withered* before your time.' There were a few sniggers. Grimble blinked, uncomprehending. The cook approached the glowing Falego. 'And if you lay so much as a finger on the Princess,' she menaced quietly, 'it won't be your thumbs I'll be cuffing in the future, d' you hear?' She unlocked the contraption that held his hands together. The young man bowed unctuously.

'What about the stranger?' chimed in Elbows Mick. 'We can't just let him sit outside all night with the beasts. It was his idea in the first place.' All turned to regard him, where he watched quietly from his spot in the corner. From the visitors came muted "ayes" of agreement. The principal servants regarded one another. The stranger continued to watch in silence. Then Grimble had an idea.

'He can wait at table,' said the caretaker. He glanced about assertively. 'The rest of us shall be his Lordship's guests.'

And so it was settled. That night, the Princess arrived for dinner.

'Good evening, Your Highness,' said Tooley, welcoming the Princess inside with a warm smile. 'Here — let me take that for you.' She helped the other out of her hooded travelling cloak and warm, winter mittens.

The guest looked about the kitchen with interested, wide eyes. A delicate frown crossed her forehead. Then she smiled to herself. 'You have a wonderful kitchen, Mistress Tooley,' she said. 'I imagined it almost just like this.' She turned to find the cook. As she did, her hair gleamed like melting honey in the firelight.

'Oh, you're most gracious, Ma'am,' replied Tooley, waving a hand bashfully. 'It's everybody's kitchen, really. Now if you'll just follow me.'

A touch bemused by Tooley's remark, but no less happy to be there, the Princess smiled and followed.

Upstairs, the corridor that led to the dining room was lined solidly either side with people. 'Good evening, Your Highness,' they all greeted in unison.

'Good evening,' the Princess responded cordially, making a great effort not to display her deepening curiosity as she walked between them. At the end of the tunnel of people, a thin, stiff man stepped forward and, breaking out a smile, presented himself.

'On his Lordship's behalf,' said the thin man, 'may I be first to impart to Your Highness what an incontrovertibly felicitous experience her expedient acceptance of his Lordship's invitation to this prandial engagement has bestowed upon this establishment in the entirety of its factions, both in the declaration of said response's intentions and indeed in its ultimate actualisation?'

The Princess blinked rapidly. 'You may,' she replied.

'I am Balthazar Grimble, the General Domo,' said Grimble, bowing until his nose almost touched the floor. 'If Your Highness so pleases,' and turning peremptorily he took three, grand strides and flung open the doors to the dining room.

Following the other's lead, the Princess walked into the blaze of firelight that came from within. No sooner had she entered the room, however, than she halted. She gazed at the spectacle before her with surprise and fascination.

The enormous hall looked like a cross between a Salvation Army surplus store and a Turkish bazaar. Folds of dark red and blue material bedecked with silver symbols and runes hung thickly from the ceiling and walls and across the far windows. The huge table was similarly covered, although its height and width varied considerable in different places, and it was set for at least twenty people. The chairs appeared to have been nailed together from old packing crates. Oil light flickered dimly and beneath the great, crumbling mantelpiece, the fire roared in its hearth like an angry dragon. 'What original decoration,' said the Princess, moving lightly forward once more into the room.

'We pride ourselves on our innovation,' said Grimble. Tooley shot him a glance. 'Uh, I mean,' stammered the caretaker, 'that is to say, his Lordship has an extraordinarily versatile mind.' The servants all smiled.

'Doesn't he just?' Their guest took in the mismatched cutlery, and the scientific beakers posing as glasses and bottles. 'Well, then,' she said with a breath. 'Where would his Lordship like me to sit? I hadn't realised there would be so many guests.'

'Oh, it's just yourself, Ma'am,' said Tooley without thinking. The Princess' eyebrows arched inquisitively. 'What I mean to say is,' backtracked the cook, 'all the rest of these folk are sort of – well – regular guests. Here, look: why don't Your Highness come and sit at the end now? His Lordship'll be here any moment. I hope.' While she had been talking, the other servants and visitors had filed quietly into the room and taken up their positions.

Uncertain, but not wishing to offend, the Princess sat

down as indicated. A clattering thump resounded through the room as twenty other people simultaneously followed suit. All eyes were on the dinner guest. All grinned like imbeciles. Not one said a word. She was just beginning to wonder whether perhaps she had stumbled upon a madhouse when a calm voice spoke beside her, breaking her thoughts.

'Would Her Highness prefer cider or sherry with her meal?' the voice said gently. Startled, the Princess looked up.

A young, bearded man with a world-worn face stood awaiting her decision. He was plainly dressed and did not look her in the eye. The Princess hesitated, suddenly unbalanced. She felt her heart beat faster. She knew she had to respond, yet the other's presence made her feel all at once light-headed – almost as though, in the middle of an ordinary hour in an ordinary day, a memory suddenly became flesh and transported her away across the fields of time. She felt the other acutely near to her. It made her feel dizzy.

'The cider is extremely good, Your Highness,' said the man helpfully when no answer came. There was a groan from the mason but he was hushed.

'Yes, thank you,' replied the Princess, recovering. 'I would love some cider.' She watched closely as he poured. The man looked only at his work. 'You're very kind,' she added.

'Ma'am.'

'Cider for all!' declared Grimble, raising his own beaker. Elbows Mick moaned again but was drowned out by a noisy cheer. Conversations started as the stranger moved away around the table once more, pouring for all.

'Excuse my curiosity, but who is that?' the Princess asked aside to Tooley. The latter had covertly produced her own private bottle of sherry.

'That? Oh – he's the, er…well, actually I mean…' The cook looked at the Princess' inquisitive but patient face and then made a decision. She leaned in conspiratorially. 'Truth be told, Ma'am, none of us right knows who he is,' she whispered. 'Arrived a few months back. I found him half froze solid in the ditch outside the gate.'

'Does he have a name?' the Princess asked, intrigued. Her eyes followed the young man as he moved.

'We just call him "the stranger",' replied Tooley, wiping her mouth. 'He don't know his name – or his age, or where he came from, or nothing.' She refilled her glass. 'But, just between you and me, Your Highness, there's something about him. If you know what I mean?'

'Yes,' said the Princess, still watching. 'I do.'

After a few minutes had passed, a shrill little voice from the far end of the table called out: 'Do you like our castle,

Your Highness?' The room hushed. The Princess squinted and at length located the angular face of Ms Fawcett.

'Very much,' the guest replied politely. 'I find it extremely' — she searched for the word — 'eclectic,' she said at last.

'Oh, bravo,' the delighted Grimble exclaimed. 'Or rather, brav*a*.' He winked.

'I designed the roof myself,' Ms Fawcett continued proudly. 'Do you like it?'

'It's very, mm…avant-garde.' The Princess nodded solemnly.

'And I did the tinsel,' put in Elbows Mick.

'Yes, well. We're not all quite sure about the tinsel.' Ms Fawcett turned her nose up. A couple of the other visitors began to argue quietly.

The Princess looked perplexed. 'So…you're all his Lordship's servants?' she asked. A few worried glances were exchanged about the table. Then there was a mutter; a few random "yeses". 'What — all of you?' More "ayes" and nods. 'And you all make plans and decisions for him and eat with him every night?'

Grimble cleared his throat. Leaning forward, he said: 'If it will aid in your elucidation, Your Highness, you might say that we are a democratic socialist oligarchic meritocracy.' He smiled odiously. 'His Lordship is extremely liberal.'

'I see.' The stranger began to bring in the food: steaming platters of meat and roasted vegetables, with assorted fruit jellies and thick gravy. It was the first proper food that had been seen in the castle for such a long time, and the rich smells were so potent, that a couple of the visitors almost swooned. Even the fussiest of eaters among the caretaker's crew began to salivate in anticipation. The stranger served the Princess first and then distributed the rest.

'Are you not eating with us — Sir?' the royal guest asked as he turned to leave the room. He stopped. Slowly, the stranger lifted his head and looked at the Princess properly for the first time.

As he gazed at her, all his senses froze. Everything around him save for her — the people, the talk, the castle, even the very air — became illusion and dissolved. Her beauty astounded him, and he felt it with the core of his being. There was no doubting that at that moment, the only true entities in that space, the only reality that could be weighed or hold any value before the eyes of the watching universe, were he and she. There was an unmistakable force that tied them to one another. It had to be experienced to be believed. All else was dust. Then he remembered that he remembered nothing.

'No, Ma'am,' he replied as the magic faded. 'I'm just the servant.' With that, he turned and walked quickly away.

'Of course,' Grimble continued to prattle as he licked a finger, 'we are also extraordinarily well-connected.'

The Princess shook the daze from her head. In spite of her racing pulse and singing nerves, she forced herself to meet the caretaker's words with civility. 'Is that so, Mr Grimble?'

'Mmm.' The other nodded, sucking. 'In fact,' he stated, with a swell of the chest, 'Seer Fanta himself is one of our most frequent visitors.' He paused and casually reached for his cider to lend the moment an extra touch of impressiveness.

His words, however, did not have the intended effect. At the mention of the Seer's name, the Princess' features hardened and her eyes narrowed. 'Are you acquainted with the mighty Seer?' continued Grimble obliviously.

'I have had the misfortune to meet Mr Fanta only once,' their guest replied tightly. 'He came to my door offering trinkets from the void and a life of unhappiness. In consequence, I gave my servants instructions never to admit either he or any of his gruesome band of swindlers ever again.'

There was absolute silence in the dining room. Grimble's blank face was frozen at mid-chew.

The Princess folded her napkin. 'Now I think I see also what has happened here,' she said. 'That charlatan has taken your Lord, too. Has he not?' There was no reply. 'Has he not?' she asked again, barely restraining her passion.

Not a person uttered a word. No one could think of a reply, stunned as they were at their guest's clarity of perception. Then Elbows Mick burped.

'I thank you for your hospitality,' said the Princess. With a courteous nod towards Tooley, she rose to leave. She did not get very far.

'Prepare ye all for the coming of the Lord!' hailed a voice from beyond the dining room. Everyone turned uncertainly. The Princess paused and frowned. Beneath their feet, the floorboards began to quiver. Then, a storm broke upon them.

With a tremendous crash the dining room doors burst open. Hauled by a perspiring Mr Fusset and one of Tooley's more unbalanced, bridge-playing friends, a gaudy chariot with mismatched wheels clattered thunderously into the room and began to perform a racing lap of the table. In the back of the chariot – in reality an old trap dragged from the woodshed and poorly painted – stood Falego. He was dressed as a bullfighter, with sword, stars, cape and all, and on his head perched a hat crammed with enough feathers to terminally embarrass a peacock. The young man stared hotly about the shocked spectators like a returning emperor as the chariot rumbled past. When the panting human mules at last reached the end of their circuit, the Spaniard leaped athletically from his charge and landed in a broad hero's pose on the table. To an assembled gasp, he whipped out his sword. Staring hungrily at the Princess, with rapacious intent he began skewering meat and vegetables left and right with his sabre, all the while advancing purposefully towards her. Eventually, he arrived. Balancing on his toes at the table's edge, and breaking out his finest porcelain smile, Falego swung the tip of the quivering weapon towards the startled face of his quarry.

Somewhat overwhelmed at the evening's latest turn, the Princess stared down at the laden offering before her. Falego leaned close to her and smiled.

'Do you kebab?'

The Princess surveyed the handsome Spaniard dubiously. 'My *Lord*?'

'Please,' returned Falego, indicating with a gleam for her to sit.

Warily, the Princess acceded.

'Everyone!' the other shouted out to the rest of the room. 'Come on! Eat, drink – laugh, if you know how. Do you think this is a wake? This is a celebration – a celebration to the arrival of exquisite beautifulness in our lives.' The table started up once more. Falego dropped casually down onto the floor and draped himself on one elbow across the space in front of the Princess.

'So,' drawled the Spaniard, displaying every shining tooth to the uncertain guest. 'What's an angel like you doing here so far from heaven?'

'Oh please.' The Princess rolled her eyes. 'If you're going to insist on being crass you might at least try to be original.'

Falego frowned. 'What you no like? You don't like it when a man make some beautiful love to you?'

'Hah!' The other laughed indignantly. 'You call that making love? I call it making a spectacle of yourself. My Lord,' she added with emphasis.

'You no like spectacle?' Falego looked wounded. 'All right. You stick around and I'll make you respectful receptacle of most expected spectacle. —acle,' he said again, confused.

'I thought you made candles,' the Princess levelled.

'Pah! Candles are for women.'

'I love candles.'

'And I love women like I love my candles, oh!' – Falego wailed – 'I miss them so much.' He bit his fist in mock injury.

The Princess frowned. 'Well...what happened?' she asked more gently.

'The customs,' replied the Spaniard, clearing imaginary

tears. 'They held my wick.'

'That's awful.'

'They had to let it go, is okay. But soon I will make more — hundreds, thousands of big, strong candles.' He mimed grotesquely. Then he switched tack. 'Do you like to dance?'

'Yes, very much, but-'

'Good. Later, we dance. I will see how you move.' He ran his dark eyes over her lithe, feminine form. 'But first' — he clapped — 'I will dance for you. Amigos!' And with that, he leaped back onto the table.

The Princess sat back on her crate, confused and not a little suspicious, as with a devilish grin fixed in her direction the Spaniard now began to flamenco. Accompanying him on an old classical guitar was the surprisingly animated Mr Fusset, who had re-emerged from his charioteering duties and played along almost entranced. The bridge-player completed the peculiar trio by banging a tambourine and occasionally shouting. The young man's bootheels pounded on the rickety table, spilling plates and beakers as he wound up into a rhythm. Everyone at the table — with the exception of the Princess and Tooley — had started to clap time, so hypnotised were they by the dancer; even, the cook noticed with astonishment, Grimble himself.

The clapping grew louder and louder, the shouts wilder and more numerous, as Falego, face twisted in dark, Latin concentration, worked his way back up along the table to where the Princess was seated. His feet moved almost too fast to be seen. The pace and the noise became dizzying. Ornaments and cutlery, plates and glasses, began to vibrate across the uneven surface and crash onto the floor, but none could take their eyes off the whirling bootheels.

The guitar stopped suddenly. Falego froze. He shot Fusset a meaningful, lightning look and then, breathing fiercely, set his sights on the bewildered guest at the table's head. Fusset backed furtively towards the wall as the Spaniard's feet began to bang and click once more. Falego inched towards her, the table beginning to shake anew. Everyone in the dining room held their breath, intent on the charm of the dance. Unnoticed by all save the dancer himself, a jar of cider had started to buzz on the rhythm of striking heels and was now creeping slowly but surely towards the Princess. The Spaniard drew near. The tempo reached its peak. Then, in a trice, the cider jar tipped and splashed all over the Princess' dress.

'Oh!' she cried out in surprise.

At that very moment, quick as you like, Fusset pulled a cord behind him. At the same instant, he stood heavily on a floorboard by his foot. As Tooley O' Marge reached up to grab the lunging Spaniard, a drape directly above her fell heavily and carried her to the floor in a flailing bundle. Falego advanced. Taking a step back, the Princess' heel struck the raised end of the floorboard. The next thing she knew, she was falling. Time slowed and swam as reaching hands and strange faces filled her vision. Then, just as she thought she would surely hit the hard, wooden floor, she felt two strong arms about her.

'Wet?' said Falego.

The Princess gasped. 'A little.'

Falego picked her off her feet as the chariot was brought around. 'I take you some place warm.'

'I'm quite warm here, thank you very much,' retorted the other with as much dignity as she could muster.

Falego gazed at her ardently. 'Why be only warm,' the Spaniard sighed, 'when God has given you so much flame?' And, swinging her up in a single, swift movement, he leaped into the chariot after her. With a whistle, they were off.

'I suppose you're going to show me your tower, now?' said the Princess, arching an eyebrow.

Falego grinned. 'Bella signorita,' he replied, 'I thought you would never ask.'

'Naturally,' said Dr Ummond, 'the impudent Spanish toad took the Princess down to his den in the basement and tried to put his grubby hands on her. Fortunately, she was indeed a dancer herself and she had two strong legs to prove it. She only needed one. The posturing Latin handbag couldn't stand straight for a week.

'After her escape, the Princess ran wildly through the castle. Most of the house was in darkness, and so seeing as she was lost she just went up and up and up, until she could go no higher. At last she came to a cold, narrow corridor. In the dim light of the Moon through the arrow slits she could just make out at its end a strong, wooden door. Standing before the door was a man...'

The man turned at her arrival. 'Sorry, I – I didn't mean to frighten you.' The Princess caught her breath.

'You didn't,' the stranger said. He smiled sadly.

Composing herself, the Princess went softly over to stand beside him.

'It's a funny thing,' the stranger continued wistfully as she looked across at him with curious eyes. 'I feel safer here than anywhere else. I don't know why.'

'Isn't it frightening not knowing anything about yourself?'

The other's smile grew broader. 'It would be foolish to be frightened of nothing,' he replied. 'Wouldn't it?'

The Princess looked at him. Then she conceded with a smile of her own. 'I suppose,' she said. Her face fell serious again. 'I know something about you, though.' The stranger regarded her warily, not understanding. 'You're a good man,' she said, quietly and in earnest. Very slowly, as though reaching out to a wounded animal, the Princess raised a small hand and gently touched his beard. She stroked it with delicate, careful fingers. Then, feeling all at once self-conscious, she let her hand drop. 'I should go now,' she said hastily and turned.

'You're soaked, Your Highness. Can I-?'

'No. Thank you.' There was a pause. 'Good night.'

'Good night, Ma'am.' The Princess moved swiftly away down the corridor. Before she reached the end, however, she stopped to look back.

'You know — every door has a key.' They held one another's eyes. Then, she smiled quickly and was gone.

10

A FTERNOON,' SAID MARCUS cheerily as he walked into No. 73 the following week.

The receptionist looked up. 'Oh. Hello, Mr Grool. You been keeping yourself well, then?'

'Very well, thank you,' replied Marcus. 'Erm — would there be any chance of a cup of tea?'

The receptionist smiled at him with her little blue eyes. 'Half a tock,' she said, pushing herself up. 'You won't believe this, but I think the kettle might have just boiled.' With a friendly wink, she disappeared through the doorway by the stairs.

In a chair beside it, Marcus suddenly noticed a figure he had not seen at first. It appeared to be a man, slumped with his very long legs straight out in front of him and snoring gently. At least, Marcus assumed it to be a man due to his smart, black suit and the elegant, silver-tipped cane that rested in a gnarled hand. The face, however, was completely obscured by a fine, wide-brimmed hat.

'Oh, thanks.' The receptionist handed Marcus his tea. 'Is he here to see the Doctor, too?' he asked, sipping.

'What, him?' The old dame chuckled. 'No, we don't see much of him these days,' she said. 'Hasn't got the energy he used to.' Her features flattened for an instant as she added quietly: 'Thank goodness.'

When he had finished, Marcus thanked her again and smiled. 'I'll just go on up as usual, shall I?' he asked. The receptionist started to nod, then she suddenly caught herself.

'Oh, wait. Lummy me, I am a forgetful old thing,' she said with a giggle. 'Now I remember: the Doctor told me to tell you once you'd finished your tea that he can't see you today 'cause he's died.'

Marcus stared. 'Because he's..?'

'You know.' The other drew a plump hand across her neck. 'Dead.'

The young man frowned and thought, stunned. 'But I mean...how did he die?' he asked softly in amazement.

'I don't know,' replied the old girl, raising her palms. 'You'll have to go and ask him yourself. I just do as the old fruitcake tells me.'

Marcus grinned enormously and took off up the stairs at a run.

'It was the shock, Grool,' said Ummond with a sly, cracked smile. He shuffled away from the window. 'Didn't have you down as a tea drinker. Something inside just keeled over from the surprise.' He mimed a heart attack.

'Well, that could've happened to me,' the patient chastised, still with a smile. 'What was I meant to learn from that anyway?'

The Doctor cackled. 'Zeeks, Grool,' he said at last. 'If you keep asking that sort of question there's a very real danger you might start to become interesting. I should have to start listening to you. That *would* be a funny thing.' Marcus demurred. 'Anyway, I think we'll leave the "Awareness of Death" discourse for another time. Let's get the living living first, shall we?'

'Yes, Doctor.'

'So,' began Ummond, smacking his lips. 'After the-'

'Doctor?'

'What did I do?'

'Sorry, it's just…' Marcus pointed. 'You haven't lit the candle.'

There on the desk, with only two hours remaining, the candle sat cold and lifeless.

'But I've got my fancy new computer,' returned the Doctor with a frown. He pulled up his sleeve. 'I can make it beep, boop and everything.'

'I'd like it all the same – if that's all right,' said Marcus.

Dr Ummond leaned forward and lit it. Outwardly, his face remained as craggy and unreadable as ever. What the other could not see as he watched, however, were the years of practice and self-discipline that prevented tears from forming in the old man's eyes at just these very moments. 'There you are, laddie,' he said, sitting back. He tapped the desk idly. Then, with a clear voice, Ummond said: 'After the flamenco fiasco, morale in the castle reached previously uncharted depths…'

'We might as well just pull the place down and finish it now,' said Balthazar Grimble as he and the others sat gloomily around the broken dining table the following morning. The caretaker scrunched despairingly at his knuckles. 'Look at us. We've nothing to live for. No friends. No books.'

'No cider,' mumbled Elbows Mick, staring miserably at an empty jar.

'I'm going to do it,' stated Grimble, standing suddenly stock still. 'Come on: who'll do it with me?' He stared about crazedly. 'All those in favour…' But no one had either the inclination or the energy to do anything.

'What's he banging on about now?' huffed Tooley O' Marge as she entered the room carrying a steaming great pot of lumpy porridge. She dumped it on an upturned crate.

'Mr Grimble wants to do himself in,' said Ms Fawcett with a bored yawn. 'I still just don't know how the Princess saw through us so easily.'

Tooley began to dish up. 'Well, that's fine by me,' she said as she served. 'Someone had better inform the great Brigadier General Domo, though, that he might hurt himself in the process.' The caretaker paled visibly.

'How is young master Falego today?' a meek Mr Fusset enquired. One of the visitor's eyes was swollen and puffed from where the cook had exacted her revenge for the netting incident.

'Young master Falego,' Tooley responded shortly, 'won't be dancing for us again for some while yet. And unless you want your face to be all matching,' she added with stomach-turning calmness, 'I'd not alert me to your presence again, Mr Fusset. Not for a few days yet, d' you understand?' She scraped the pot and took a seat.

'Quite right, Miss O' Marge,' concurred Grimble, who had reconsidered his suicide scheme in lieu of breakfast and undamaged skin. He glared across the table at Fusset. 'Little Judas,' he hissed.

'You seemed to be rather enjoying yourself last night,' put in the tambourine beater in the other's defence. There were murmurs of agreement.

'I recall the Princess was leaving anyway,' said another, 'on account of the mention of a certain name.' A ripple of assent now ran through the dining room.

Grimble looked about, stupefied. Every face was on him. Finally, he gathered himself. 'That's it, is it? That's the gratitude I get? After ten years. Ten years of entirely selfless support; of leadership and nurture.'

'I don't wish to go bursting your bubble, now,' interrupted Tooley, 'but you couldn't support a bird bath if they scooped out your head and covered you in concrete.'

Grimble's eyes widened so far in outrage that the tops of his eyeballs became visible. 'Right,' he declared, rising abruptly. 'That is the final straw and I am a camel.' A few of those gathered exchanged glances. 'What is more,' he continued, 'I have had enough of this desert, this, this...*drought*. It is quite plain that none of you has the requisite imagination to get us out of this predicament. Therefore, it appears that once again our future welfare shall be upon my shoulders. I'm going to do something that'll stump the lot of you. And I know just who is going to help me.' With that, and a smug little smile, he headed for the door.

The remainder of the room now regarded one another, baffled and not a little curious at the caretaker's sudden change in temperament.

'What are you going to do, Mr Grimble?' enquired Ms Fawcett as he reached the doorway.

Grimble looked casually over his shoulder. 'I am going to liberate the treasure we need. The same treasure that has been in our grasp all along.' There were confused glances. 'I'm going to open the tower.'

An hour later, the entire household had packed itself with excited anticipation before the solid, oak wood door. 'Make way! Make way for the magnificent Fanta,' came the officious voice of the interpreter from behind them. All squeezed back against the walls as the ever-smiling magician – grown markedly rotund on the profits of his plunderings – swished his way ceremoniously towards the locked portal.

'Your masterfulness,' seeped Grimble, bowing.

The Seer nodded. He gabbled to the interpreter. This latter turned to the caretaker. 'Ninety percent of the contents on entry,' he rattled off flatly, then smiled. 'No cash – no smash.'

Tooley and Grimble conferred hurriedly as everyone else strained their ears. 'Sixty,' announced Grimble eventually with authority.

'Eighty,' replied the interpreter.

'Seventy.'

'Eighty-five.'

'Done,' returned Grimble triumphantly and pointed at the door.

All stood back as Seer Fanta stepped up into position. His eyes narrowed as he surveyed the woodwork. Then, with his habitual display of extraordinary, mystical powers, the conjuror summoned up his strength and kicked at the door with all his might.

The door did not budge.

Scowling and muttering to himself, the magician drew back his foot and, with a giant yell, kicked again.

It did not so much as shudder.

Hobbling somewhat, the now cursing Fanta went and had indecipherable words with his interpreter. After several, intense moments, the interpreter approached the caretaker.

'The Seer believes that this door has been placed under a charm,' he said to heated whisperings all along the corridor. 'He says,' the interpreter continued, 'that according to rare and most magical books which the Seer alone can understand, the charm may be broken only by the power of the mind borne on the tide of the emotions.' Everyone conferred.

'Tide of the... Well, I say,' uttered Grimble, wiping his forehead.

'The Seer suggests,' finished the interpreter, 'that in order to open the door we harness your own extraordinary mind and join it with the force of the deep swell that rises in Miss O' Marge and her friends.' He smiled at them.

Grimble coughed importantly. 'Yes, that does appear to make sense,' he agreed. 'Now, how does one-?' But before he could finish, hands were upon him. A second later he was hoisted off his feet.

'Stop!' cried Grimble. 'What are you doing? Have you lost all your reason?'

'I think I understood the Seer perfectly,' replied Tooley as, between herself and her visitors, Balthazar Grimble was turned horizontal in mid-air and his terrified head aimed directly at the door. 'Are we ready, ladies?' huffed the cook. Everyone stood back. 'Right: one...'

'Help!' the caretaker screamed. He struggled uselessly as he was swung back by several strong women. 'This is not a rational way of behaviour!'

'Two,' grated Tooley. The caretaker's body gained momentum.

'You don't know what you're doing!' he shrieked. 'This is not how it's done! I have an eggshell skull!' Seer Fanta and his crew grinned greedily.

'And-'

'Stop.'

The caretaker's body paused. It hovered at the top of its final swing. Every head turned; every head, that is, except for Grimble's, which was frozen in fright. Eventually, he too managed to open one eye and take a look behind.

With his inverted vision, Grimble watched as the crowd in the corridor behind him parted and a figure approached between them. At first, all he could see was a pair of legs and two muddy feet. Then, the knees bent and a face appeared before him. It was a bearded face. It regarded him for a moment with piercing eyes. Then it smiled.

'Hello there, Grimble,' said the stranger. 'Am I imagining things, or are you not entirely happy?'

Overcome with shock and incomprehension, the human battering ram that was Balthazar Grimble sighed weakly and fainted.

The stranger straightened. 'What are you all doing here?' he demanded.

Releasing the unconscious caretaker, Tooley stepped nervously forward. 'We was just trying to do something that might help us,' she explained, wringing her hands. 'Getting into the tower might be our last hope. We haven't got nothing else.'

'That door,' said the stranger, 'can be opened only with a

key. And only then by a key in the hand of a Lord.'

'How do you know?' piped a suspicious Ms Fawcett. There were murmurs of agreement.

The young man regarded them. 'I just do.' He waited in case any should decide to challenge his conviction. None did. He turned to Seer Fanta. 'And you,' he said, his eyes narrowing, 'I have heard your language before.' The stranger advanced on the recoiling magician. 'I have heard your words translated into tales of riches and discoveries beyond any man's dreams; tales of islands and adventures just around the corner, waiting to be found by brave and resourceful travellers. And when I heard you speaking that language again just now, I began to remember. I should perhaps thank you for that. But I will not. For those words are not real, any more than the treasures they fail to speak of. Your language is nothing but an illusion, an empty babbling from the void. It brings only oblivion, suffering and death. You cannot speak because there is no substance but just the imaginings of empty desires. You' – the stranger glared – 'do not even exist.'

To the astonishment of every person standing there in that narrow corridor, as the stranger finished speaking an incredible thing now happened: Seer Fanta began to shrink. First his hands grew smaller and retreated back into his magician's sleeves; then his feet disappeared from his curly-toed shoes. Finally, with an expression of silent fear and loathing, his entire face and head began to diminish and receded before the stranger's gaze of fire. At last, there was nothing left of the great illusionist but an empty pile of clothes on the floor.

The interpreter stared in horror at the spot where he had stood. 'Master!' he began to wail. He was about to fall to his knees when he felt a strong hand on his shoulder. Slowly, he turned.

'You,' said the stranger quietly, 'are the worst of them all.' Abruptly, the interpreter's visage changed. What had seconds before appeared to be genuine grief was replaced by genuine hatred. He stared for an instant longer at the face of the one who had exposed him. Then, followed by the remnants of his renegade mob, he wheeled and strode away.

The stranger looked about him.

Twenty faces gawped back, utterly dumbfounded. Then, there was a movement in the corner.

'Oh, my head,' said Balthazar Grimble. He rose shakily. Then he stopped. He regarded the motionless corridor with suspicion. 'Did something happen?'

'I'm telling you: it's *him*,' Tooley O' Marge whispered hoarsely. Servants and visitors alike were clustered outside the entrance to the study, where the stranger now stood before the portrait on the far wall.

Grimble sniffed indignantly. 'Murdering one of the finest, wisest men in the whole world is hardly conduct worthy of a Lord. Besides,' he added, 'if it is indeed his Lordship, which I cannot dare believe it is, then why doesn't he know where the key to the tower is?'

"Cause he don't remember himself, you great treacle pudding,' replied the cook. 'Now hush up. I'm going to try something.' Tooley cleared her throat and prepared herself. Putting on a broad smile, she entered the study. She went over and stood behind the stranger. 'My Lord?' The other seemed not to hear her. He continued to gaze at the picture as though in a trance. She tried again. 'Excuse me – my *Lord*?'

He span around. 'Oh, Tooley. Sorry, I – I must have been daydreaming.' They regarded one another for a moment, smiling awkwardly. 'Well then,' the stranger said at length. 'I'd better go and see to the beasts.' Tooley's face fell, as too did her heart, as he walked out of the room.

At dinner that evening, she tried again. 'Here we are, then,' she announced. She was back in her old cook's outfit, filthy apron and all, and she carried a large pot. 'Thought we'd have a change tonight. Been a while since we had dumplings.'

She and Grimble sat side by side and watched the stranger intently as he ate. There was no discernible reaction.

'I never understood why his Lordship liked these things so much anyway,' commented the caretaker disdainfully.

'You wouldn't,' returned Tooley. She was concentrating on the young man's every move. 'That's why you'd have made such an 'opeless battering ram.' She looked across slyly.

'No thanks to you.' Her companion sniffed. 'I don't know what got into you to even consider such an idea.'

'Just seemed like a good idea at the time,' the cook shrugged. 'Anyway, I used to be good at cracking eggs.' Grimble regarded her. 'Oh, come on now, Balthazar. Cheer up. We might have this place right again soon if we're lucky.' They continued to observe.

'Tooley: do you really think it might be his Lordship?' Grimble asked. All at once, his voice was abnormally devoid of pretension.

'Why, yes,' replied the cook. 'Course I do. I can tell these things.' She stopped and looked at her fellow servant. 'You do want him back again – don't you?'

The caretaker's forehead creased. He smiled up at her, all at once resembling nothing more nor less than a small child. 'Yes,' he said simply. 'More than anything.'

'Excellent dumplings, Miss Tooley.' The stranger nodded across at her. Then, he began to clear away the dishes.

'I don't' know what else to do,' sighed the cook, crestfallen. She returned the other's smile weakly.

Beside her, a small light flickered on in Grimble's eyes. 'I think I may have an idea,' he said.

11

THE FOLLOWING DAY, Tooley made a routine call to the pen down by the gate. As she was leaving, she turned and said casually, 'Oh, by the way – Mr Grimble and me have had a thought. Regarding the Princess.' At that word, the young man's head snapped up from where he was feeding the pigs. 'We wondered if you couldn't lend us a hand a bit later,' the cook continued. 'In the study?'

'Yes. Yes, of course,' he replied.

'Righty ho, then. Till later.' As she trundled back along the driveway to the castle, Tooley bit on a carrot and chuckled to herself. 'Oldest one in the book,' she laughed.

'Hello?'

'Ah, there you are.' Tooley rose from the study bureau.

It was early evening and the castle was quiet. The stranger came in and waited. 'Now,' explained the cook, 'what me and Mr Grimble was thinking is that we ought to write the Princess a letter, apologising for...well, you know: for the other night.'

'A good idea,' the stranger agreed, nodding.

'Thing is,' went on Tooley, appearing anxious, 'Mr Grimble's right busy today and I'm not so very good with words, so we was wondering if you couldn't write it for us?' She looked at him hopefully.

The stranger smiled sadly. 'You forget that I can neither read nor write,' he said. The other's face dropped doubly. He added: 'But if you liked, I could always dictate for you.'

Tooley pondered for an instant. Then her ruddy features lit up. 'That's a corking idea,' she beamed. 'Now just you stay right there,' and she flapped over to the bureau and grabbed a sheaf of paper and a pen. She settled herself before the desk. 'Right, then,' she exhaled, dipping the nib in the inkpot. 'How will it start?'

The stranger thought. '"Your Highness",' he began, focusing. '"I write to you on behalf of the whole castle..."'

'"Behalf...whole...castle",' repeated the cook. 'Yes?'

'"To express my profoundest apologies..."'

'"Profoundest..." How do you spell "apologies"?'

'Um: *a-p-o-l-o-g-i-e-s*,' replied the stranger at once.

Tooley smiled. 'Go on.'

'"Apologies for the unbecoming and no doubt distressing behaviour…"'

'"No…doubt…" Has "distressing" got one "s" in the middle or two?'

'Two. "The distressing behaviour of…"' The stranger stopped. Then he frowned. He looked at Tooley. 'I can spell,' he said. He thought for a moment more. Then the corner of his mouth turned up. 'Tooley, I…I can spell,' he breathed.

The cook was near bursting with delight.

The stranger ran across to the bureau and took the pen from her. He scribbled furiously. 'I can write!' he cried. 'Tooley, I can… Look!' Words started to pour from the pen. He dropped it suddenly and, with admirable strength, picked the glowing cook up off the floor and swung her around in his arms. As he did, Balthazar Grimble, who in time-honoured fashion had been listening at the door throughout, jumped into the room in astonished delight.

'Your Lordship!' the caretaker cried. 'It's you, Sir! It's really you!'

The stranger released the swooning cook. 'But – how can you be sure?' he asked, puzzled.

'Oh, bless me,' exclaimed Tooley, reeling. She reached into a drawer in the desk. 'We don't need any more convincing,' she said. 'But if you think it'll help, look at these here.' She handed him a thick fan of letters.

The stranger took them unsurely. 'These are... I wrote these?' Grimble picked up the piece of paper on which the young man had just been writing. The stranger looked at it. The hand was identical. He blinked. Then he smiled. 'I wrote these,' he said, as though awaking from a dream. 'I remember: from The Brave Seadreamer. So long ago. So long, now. I remember it all. And you kept them.' The cook blushed. 'Tooley – Grimble,' breathed the stranger. He looked with clearness and wonder at the space in the study where his servants stood clinging to one another in joy. 'I'm home.'

There was a suspended moment as each looked to the other and back again. Then the Lord let out a great yell and ran over and hugged them both. The three of them laughed and wept for a minute where they held each other, turning as one in the centre of that bare and mouldering room. At last, they released one another.

'Go and fetch the other servants,' said the Lord. 'No visitors, mind,' he added.

Grimble, glowing, bowed excitedly and shot out of the room as fast as his bandy legs would carry him. The Lord turned to Tooley. 'And you, my faithful cook,' he said with a glint in his eye. 'Do you still have the candle? The one I 'gave to you, the day that I left?'

'Oh, yes I do, my Lord,' replied Tooley, beaming. She added: 'And it's a good thing Mr Grimble's gone n' all. You'll never guess where I hid it.' And plunging a chubby hand down into her enormous bosom, she retrieved the candle in its faded wrapping paper.

The Lord grinned. 'Thank you, Tooley,' he said fondly.

'Safest place in the whole land,' said the cook proudly. 'More's the pity.'

Minutes later, the Lord and his five servants stood united once more in a group around the study bureau. On the desk, with its lurid, swirling colours, was the candle. The Lord looked to each of the others in turn. 'Ready?' They nodded. He searched out a match. Then, with a brisk strike, he set it to the wick. There was a loud fizz.

A second later came a flash followed by a colossal explosion. Everyone dove for the floor as with a terrific *Bang!* the candle flew apart, scattering bright and burning coloured wax off in all directions. Moments later, the wax unaccountably burned away and, as if by magic, vanished into thin air. All slowly regained their feet. There, lying on the desk, they saw what had been locked away inside for over ten, long years.

The Lord approached. With excited but sure fingers, he took the key in his hand. He studied it carefully, feeling its weight, its ridges and contours, as familiar as his own skin — the beating of his own heart in his chest. He knew at that moment that he would never be parted with it again. He clasped it tightly. Then he grinned and rushed towards the door.

'Your Lordship,' cried Tooley. 'What about the letter to the Princess?'

The Lord turned. 'Tooley,' he said: 'Fix us up a mountain of dumplings big enough to lose a giraffe in. Grimble: get rid of those visitors. Ten years is long enough for any house visit. Nitch, you set all the fires blazing and Elbows Mick, get up on that roof and put it back how it was, turrets and all. Oh, and lose the tinsel.'

'Yes, Sir,' said the mason with vigour in his eyes once more.

'As for you…' The Lord turned to Falego. 'You get back downstairs where you belong. I may pay you a visit later, but first' — he winked — 'I've got a call to make.' And with that, he bounded out of the study, down along the long, narrow corridor and finally to that indomitable, oak wood door.

Carefully, he inserted the key in the lock and turned it in the way only he knew. With a *clack* the bolt went back and in seconds the Lord was back in his beloved tower. It was just as he had left it and there were candles absolutely everywhere. He went about and lit every single one before running over to look through his telescope.

From atop her castle on the far side of the valley, the Princess saw the light where it shone like a beacon out across the dark forests of Ude. Rushing to the window, she leaned out into the breeze and let the golden glow fill her heart. There would be no more dark and silent nights of staring alone at the Moon from now on. She knew now that finally her Lord had truly returned.

'Don't you just love a tear-jerker ending?' said Dr Ummond to his patient.

Marcus smiled. He looked at his hands and thought. 'Is that really it, Doctor?' he asked. He looked up. 'There isn't a bit more?'

Ummond raised his eyebrows. 'Well, there's the usual, happy cliché, but it might just make you puke, Grool.' He realised his accidental pun and laughed softly. 'Sorry about that.'

Marcus remained unruffled. 'I'd like to hear it anyway – if that's all right?'

'Zooks! I'll be up for one of those Oscar thingammies next. Very well. What happened after that was that obviously the Princess fell madly in love with the dashing, intelligent, sensitive young hero – and vice versa, naturally

— and so they got hitched. Their respective masons moved the castles next to one another, and the towers were joined at the top. And thus they lived happily — barring the occasional spat which was invariably won by the Princess — ever after. Ta-da!'

Marcus nodded thoughtfully. 'Did the Duke ever come back?'

Ummond sighed. There was a strange, genuinely sad expression in his sea-green gaze as he said: 'No, the Duke never returned. Nor most of the other Lords. Nor the King.' He paused. 'The land of Ude became by and large rather a shadow of what it was meant to be. But you never know.' Dr Ummond looked out through the window towards the world outside. 'Some day.'

'And the candle?' said Marcus quietly. 'What did the Lord put in the candle to make it burn so fast?'

'In that candle,' replied Ummond, 'the Lord put all his illusions.'

'And in the other? The one that shone in the tower all those years?'

The Doctor gleamed. 'How's the teacher?' he asked, taking a breath and stretching his old bones. He glanced at the candle on the desk. The flame was just shy of reaching the figure "X". He looked back to Marcus and held his regard.

'She's all right,' the young man was saying. 'I think me being here helps her almost as much as it does me.'

Ummond waved a skinny hand. 'I can't help you, I told you. But if you're lucky, you might just help each other. Eh?'

Marcus smiled. 'Thank you.'

'Don't mention it. Now, there was just one other thing...' muttered the Doctor to himself. With a faint crackle, the top two points of the figure "X" dissolved as vapour into the study. 'No — forgotten it,' Ummond said. 'Oh! Drat and blast, would you look at that? Another charity case. You're going to be naked soon at this rate, Edmond.' He leaned forward and hastily batted out the flame.

Marcus reached into his coat pocket. 'I'm going to pay you,' he said earnestly.

'No you're not.'

'Really.' He held the cheque out towards the Doctor. Ummond pushed it away. 'Look, Doctor,' Marcus began, but the other grabbed his hand and all of a sudden stared at him with such a peculiar regard that he fell silent.

'Put it towards something that matters,' said the old man intently.

Marcus frowned. 'But I thought-'

'Marcus,' said the Doctor. 'Trust me on this one, eh?'

Quite bewildered and mumbling his thanks, the other withdrew his hand. Ummond smiled. Then he leaned down behind the desk and retrieved something from a drawer. With a grimace, he closed the drawer and put the object on the desk. It was a large, oblong shaped package. 'If you want to pay me,' continued the Doctor, 'take that home with you. You'll know when to use it.' Marcus took the parcel unsurely.

'Thank you,' he said again. There was a long silence as he simply sat there and stared, thinking. Eventually, the Doctor squinted and asked:

'Are you all right, laddie? You look like you just swallowed a thistle or something.'

The young man looked up. He smiled quickly. 'No. It's just...' He waved it away. 'It doesn't matter.'

'Come on: spit it out, man,' insisted Ummond, his white eyebrows knitting together. 'You might get some of that wonderful "free advice" rubbish.' He waited.

'It's just,' said Marcus again. 'Well. It's just that...I think I'm only just beginning to really see – about the castle, I mean,' he clarified, looking up. 'And if that's what I am, then I think it's been in a very bad way for quite some time. Can it really be mended?' Marcus asked hopefully.

'But for sure, laddie,' replied the other man fondly. 'If that's what you really want.'

'I've begun to get the feeling,' Marcus continued thoughtfully, 'that actually, I hardly know myself at all.' He studied his hands. He remembered thinking that he might have never even noticed them before in his entire life. He looked up.

The Doctor's face had grown wide with surprise. The old man stared at him for a few moments longer. Then, he fell back into his chair and began to chuckle merrily. 'My, my,' said Ummond to himself. He sucked at his tongue. 'Marcus Grool. Is that a fact?'

Marcus Grool stepped out of the door of No. 73 Ludswick Road with the air of one to whom has just been given the book containing all the secrets of the Universe – written in Mandarin Chinese. He descended the steps slowly, deep in thought, and looked one last time up and down the high street as he began to walk. At the end of the road was the tavern, The Brave Seadreamer, with its black beams and whitewashed walls, and then across from him now as he passed by on the other side was Mr Meztchek, the watchmaker. The cobbler's, the confectionary; bookbinder and tailor's. Butcher and baker. Marcus turned as he heard a door open beside him.

At the entrance to No. 75, a group of young students was coming out of the dance school. As they left, laughing and talking hurriedly, an elegant lady with silver hair appeared behind them in the doorway. She stood perfectly still and watched them go, her poise at once proud yet natural. Indeed, so powerful was the sense of agelessness and control she conveyed to the onlooker that Marcus at once halted in his stride. Then, as though she had been aware of his presence all along, the woman turned gracefully to the bewildered young man and smiled. Marcus smiled back. A moment later, he frowned again as, with a twirl, she disappeared inside.

Marcus shook his head. The incident had given him another of those déjà-vu feelings in his stomach. His eyes moved, as though pulled by some strange but potent force, across to the big, brass plaque on the side of the building. He had not taken it in fully before. The plaque read: "The Princess Drummond Dance Academy".

Marcus stared. He looked suddenly up towards the roof, and to the unusual conservatory that bridged the two addresses. Heart racing, he turned and at a run went back up the steps to No. 73. He looked once more as though for the first time at the door register.

Below the Doctor's name at the top were five other bells, all with names beside them. Reading down, they were: "Balthazar Grimble; Tooley O'Marge; Elbows Mick; Patterson Nitch," and finally, somewhat scuffed, the single name: "Falego".

Marcus' breathing trebled with an unknown sense of excitement. He raised a finger and was just about to push the bell by the Doctor's name when a shout behind him in the street made him spin around.

Several people had gathered on the pavement. They were laughing and pointing to something above him on the building. Marcus blinked. Stepping back, he turned to follow their gaze.

On the first floor windowsill of No. 73, Dr Edmond Ummond, eminent quack, was to the sound of some far-off, invisible Celtic pipes dancing a jig. Naked. As in: completely and fantastically stark naked. His old wizened, pink bottom jostled dubiously about the place as its owner hopped and turned.

'We-hee!' he cried out in joy. Some of the bystanders began to applaud. Across the road, Mr Meztchek smiled and shook his head. Edmond Ummond twisted around to look over his shoulder.

'Zooks! What are you still doing here?' he called down to the smiling young man who stood below him in his winter coat, clutching a parcel. 'Don't you know when it's time to go home, Grool?'

The other looked about himself and then raised his eyebrows, as though to signify that the world was all most bewildering to him just at this moment, if nonetheless hopeful.

The Doctor's sea-green eyes twinkled fondly. 'Go on, man,' he said so that only Marcus could hear him: 'Go home. Go and find your oats.'

*   *   *

When Elizabeth returned to the apartment that evening, cold and exhausted after another long day at school, Marcus was waiting for her. As she came in, she found him standing in front of the counter that divided the sitting room and kitchen. He had an unusual expression on his face. Elizabeth put down her bags and removed her high heels in the doorway, puzzled. 'Hello, Beth,' Marcus said.

'Hello.' She shook down her frizzy hair. Then she looked at him suspiciously. 'What are you hiding?' she asked curiously, coming slowly forward.

'Oh, just. Nothing really.'

The other went around him. 'You've made dinner,' she exclaimed. 'And wine, and candles – did you get another job?'

'No,' replied Marcus, shifting. 'I mean, I will get another one, of course,' he added, seeing his girlfriend's sympathetic expression. 'But this isn't really about that.'

Elizabeth's face assumed amused perplexity once more. 'Marcus Grool, what are you up to?' She put one hand to her hip.

'Well, actually, I really just wanted to say I'm sorry,' he said at last, not quite able to look her in the eye. 'Sorry – and thank you. And…well, assuming you still want to hang around, of course, I'm going to need your help.' As he finished, he looked up.

Elizabeth's face had softened. Suddenly, her shoulders were relaxed, her mouth curved gently, and it appeared as though a great weight had been lifted. They looked truthfully at one another for the first time in an age. 'I think I'm starting to see,' Marcus began again, but Elizabeth stopped him. She went over and put her arms around her boyfriend.

'It's all right,' she said, laying her head against his chest. 'You'll do, Marcus Grool.' He hugged her back. 'You'll do.'

They stood there together for some minutes. Neither spoke a word. There was nothing that needed saying. Then, eventually, Elizabeth noticed the package on the coffee table. 'What's that?' she asked.

'Ah, yes.' Breaking from her gently, Marcus went to fetch it. 'Dr Ummond gave me this when I left. I wanted to open it with you.' He picked it up. 'I've really no idea,' he said, answering the other's glance.

With Elizabeth looking on, he pulled off the wrapping paper to reveal a box. It was of the size and shape that one might ordinarily expect to a find a bottle of whisky inside. Shrugging, Marcus opened the lid and reached in a hand. What he brought out was not whisky. It was something even more precious.

'It's a candle,' said Elizabeth with innocent surprise.

'Yes. It certainly is,' said Marcus, beaming. The candle was large and red, and had been so designed that it resembled an enormous cylinder of thick, strawberry jam.

Elizabeth sniffed. 'It even smells of it,' she said, laughing. 'Shall we light it?'

Marcus regarded the wonderful present in his hand. 'I don't think so,' he said. He smiled at his girlfriend. 'Not yet.' Turning the candle all around, his eye caught sight of a small, gold sticker on the bottom. Written across it were the words: *Made with love.*

Marcus Grool drew in a long, deep, happy breath and let it go slowly. 'Not just yet.'

Back in his study and fully clothed once more, Edmond Ummond was packing up for the evening. He put a hand to his white shock of hair as though trying to remember something, then began to look through his desk drawers. He paused for a second as he opened the one that contained all the miniscule wheels and cogs of the old pocket watch. He allowed himself a small chuckle. That watch had never worked. It never would. And the reason it would never work was because it was not *one* watch but a complete jumble of several different mechanisms for which Mr Meztchek had no further use. Ummond closed the drawer, and in the one above it found what he had been looking for: his matches.

He removed the small stub of wax that had been the candle he had used with Marcus. Holding his back with a skinny arm, he went stiffly over to the wooden chest by the door. 'I dunno, Edmond,' he said to himself as he lifted the lid. 'Dancing about naked on the windowsill. There'll be rumours flying about tomorrow that you've been taking that Niagra stuff.' He tossed the stub onto a pile of dozens that was already in the chest. A sign beneath the lid read: *For recycling*. He let it drop with a thump.

Next, he approached the tall closet that stood against the adjacent wall. Reaching out a long, thin finger he flipped the latch and stood back. The door swung slowly open on its hinges. Inside, racked up on their cases as though in a jeweller's shop window, were dozens and dozens of watches. The Doctor surveyed them for a moment. His perfect memory remembered every single face, and every single time. He reached for the one now on his wrist that Marcus had given him the week before. He was about to unfasten it when he paused. He looked down at the digital numbers ticking by. Then he smiled, and gently re-closed the closet door.

'Hah!' exclaimed Ummond, returning to the desk. 'Got to you after all, eh, you sentimental old goat?' Striking a match, he lit all five candles that stood in the silver candelabra on the desk and picked it up. With a final look about, he went to the small bathroom door in the corner of the study and then flipped out the light. The soft, golden glow from the candles shone across the Doctor's features. 'Zeeks squeaks, my boy.' He clicked his tongue. Then he went through and closed the bathroom door.

At the far end of the bathroom was another door. The Doctor now proceeded through this also and, closing it behind him, entered a dark, narrow corridor. The light in his hand moved flickering along the passageway walls like a lantern's as he ambled down it, his old heels clipping sharply in accompaniment beneath. After a turn in the corridor, he finally reached the end. Swapping the candelabra in his hands, he reached inside his jacket and pulled out a large, iron key that hung from a chain about his neck. The Doctor inserted it carefully into the lock of the oak wood door that stood before him. With a *clack* the bolt drew back. He replaced the key and then gently turned the great, brass handle. As he did so, warm light filtered down from above, illuminating the spiral stairs before him.

Edmond Ummond chuckled to himself as he stepped into the stairwell. 'All right, my love,' he said quietly. He began to close the door behind him. 'I'm coming. I'm coming.'